HUNTING THE BIRD OF PREY ...

Two of the four guards dropped to one knee and sprayed the ridge in Carter's direction with their rifles. The other two, one of them the woman, raced to the flanks, firing on the run.

The engine was roaring now and the rotors were picking up speed.

Carter sighted in on the pilot's head. It was a tough shot, almost impossible. The slugs from the two kneeling guards were kicking up sand all around Carter's head and the chopper was moving, lifting off the desert floor.

Wisely, the pilot was jiggling the machine from side to side as he got lift. El Adwan had brought his own rifle into play and was firing at the orange spurts that Ami's Ingram made in the night.

Then Carter got some peace and quiet. Ami had zeroed in on the two squatting guards. With a fanning burst he had raked them, sending them both flying backward to land, very dead, spread-eagled in the sand.

It was the lull the Killmaster needed. He sighted in . . .

NICK CARTER IS IT!

FROM THE NICK CARTER
KILLMASTER SERIES

THE ALGARVE AFFAIR

THE ANDROPOV FILE

THE ASSASSIN CONVENTION

ASSIGNMENT: RIO

THE BERLIN TARGET

BLOOD OF THE FALCON

BLOOD OF THE SCIMITAR

BLOOD RAID

BLOOD ULTIMATUM

BLOODTRAIL TO MECCA

THE BLUE ICE AFFAIR

THE BUDAPEST RUN

CARIBBEAN COUP

CIRCLE OF SCORPIONS

CROSSFIRE RED

THE CYCLOPS CONSPIRACY

DAY OF THE MAHDI

THE DEATH DEALER

DEATH HAND PLAY

DEATH ISLAND

DEATH ORBIT

DEATH SQUAD

THE DEATH STAR AFFAIR

DEATHSTRIKE

DRAGONFIRE

THE DUBROVNIK MASSACRE

EAST OF HELL

THE EXECUTION EXCHANGE

THE GOLDEN BULL

HOLY WAR

KILLING GAMES

THE KILLING GROUND

THE KREMLIN KILL

LAST FLIGHT TO MOSCOW

THE LAST SAMURAI

THE MACAO MASSACRE

THE MASTER ASSASSIN

THE MAYAN CONNECTION

MERCENARY MOUNTAIN

NIGHT OF THE CONDOR

NIGHT OF THE WARHEADS

THE NORMANDY CODE

NORWEGIAN TYPHOON

OPERATION PETROGRAD

OPERATION SHARKBITE

THE PARISIAN AFFAIR

THE POSEIDON TARGET

PRESSURE POINT

PURSUIT OF THE EAGLE

THE REDOLMO AFFAIR

REICH FOUR

RETREAT FOR DEATH

THE SAMURAI KILL

SAN JUAN INFERNO

THE SATAN TRAP

SIGN OF THE COBRA

SLAUGHTER DAY

SOLAR MENACE

THE STRONTIUM CODE

THE SUICIDE SEAT

TARGET RED STAR

THE TARLOV CIPHER

TERMS OF VENGEANCE

THE TERROR CODE

TERROR TIMES TWO

TIME CLOCK OF DEATH

TRIPLE CROSS

TUNNEL FOR TRAITORS

TURKISH BLOODBATH

THE VENGEANCE GAME

WAR FROM THE CLOUDS

WHITE DEATH

THE YUKON TARGET

ZERO-HOUR STRIKE FORCE

DEATHSTRIKE

KILL MASTER NICK CARTER

JOVE BOOKS, NEW YORK

DEATHSTRIKE

A Jove Book / published by arrangement with
The Condé Nast Publications, Inc.

PRINTING HISTORY
Jove edition / April 1988

ISBN: 0-515-09519-2

Jove Books are published by The Berkley Publishing Group,
200 Madison Avenue, New York, New York 10016.
The name "JOVE" and the "J" logo
are trademarks belonging to Jove Publications, Inc.

PRINTED IN THE UNITED STATES OF AMERICA

10 9 8 7 6 5 4 3 2 1

Dedicated to the men of the
Secret Services of the
United States of America

ONE

The morning sky grew from black to gray over the English countryside as the Pan Am 747 hummed toward Heathrow Airport.

From a seat in the first-class section, a trim, rugged-looking man, wearing a dour expression, a tan suede jacket, and a three-day growth of beard, managed a smile as the knockout stewardess approached checking each passenger's seat belt.

When she reached him, she leaned over to whisper in his ear. "I'm sorry you weren't able to get any sleep, Mr. Carter."

The powerful broad shoulders shrugged in the expensive jacket. "Comes with the territory, darlin'. What's the little bastard doing now?"

The girl managed a weak smile and swallowed hard. "He just went to sleep. Wouldn't you know it."

"Yeah, wouldn't you."

The little bastard referred to was a five-year-old in the seat in front of Carter. He had started screaming the moment the wheels had lifted off the runway at Kennedy, and he hadn't stopped all the way across the Atlantic. His total vocabulary consisted of two words—"I want"— and when he didn't get, he screamed all the louder.

When the mother, a Fifth Avenue type wearing enough ice to chill a year's martinis, wasn't coddling, she was ignoring him.

Once, Carter leaned forward. "Madam, do you know what the word discipline means?"

"I have no idea what you are talking about."

"Your child."

"I paid for this seat. I paid for my son's seat. I wish you would mind your own business."

Carter wanted to say, *Lady, do you know who I am? My name is Nicholas Carter. I work for a man named David Hawk, who runs a very quiet organization in Washington, D.C. This organization specializes in termination . . . that means killing people. And I'm their top gun. Right now, lady, I'm on my way to London to kill a man. I've been looking for the son of a bitch for three months all over the damn world. I just spent two weeks chasing him all over South America, and when I found him, he was the wrong guy. But this guy was just as bad as the guy I was hunting, so I just went ahead and offed him. And do you know what, lady? What I'd like to do right now is off your kid. No, better yet, I'd like to off you, just to keep in practice, so to speak.*

But he didn't.

Instead he'd said, "I see," and sat back, sighing.

When the flight attendant passed by again, he caught her elbow. "Excuse me . . ."

"Yes, sir?"

"Could you be a true Samaritan and slip me about three of those little plastic bundles of joy?"

"Chivas Regal?" she asked, grinning.

"Dandy."

She was back in thirty seconds and dropped the miniatures in his lap. "On the house."

"Your sainted mother is very proud of you," Carter replied, popping one and slipping the other two into his jacket pocket for the hard times ahead.

Under the harsh glare of the overhead reading light, the hard lines of his face, the broad forehead, the straight nose, and the strong, arrogant jawline seemed to relax as he took a nip. Even the blackness in his dark eyes mellowed a little.

He ran his hand through his unruly black hair and sighed again.

Seven hours earlier he had gotten off a plane from Buenos Aires, fully intending to cab right to his Georgetown digs, shower, and fall into bed for twenty-four hours.

No such luck.

An auburn-haired beauty with body curves not yet invented by geometry had met him at baggage claim. Her name was Ginger Batemen, and she was David Hawk's right hand. The moment he saw the bag in her hand he knew he was in trouble.

"That's my spare bag," he groaned.

"Oh, so correct, world traveler. I'm to take your other one back to your apartment."

"Why?"

"Here is your shuttle ticket to Kennedy. It leaves in fifteen minutes. Here is your Pan Am ticket. It leaves in an hour and a half. You'll just make it."

"Make it to where."

"London."

"I don't want to go to London. I want to go to Georgetown."

"You have to go to London," Batemen said patiently. "They have a new line on *him*."

Carter lowered his voice. "Everybody in the world has a fucking line on *him*. Do you know what I've just been through?"

She nodded. "We got your taped report on the wire. Have a nice trip."

"Wait a minute . . ."

"Yes?"

"Where do I go when I get there?"

"Someone is meeting you. Her name is Christine."

"Bully, very bully."

Carter finished the scotch as the plane touched down. Just as it hit the gate, he was the first one up and forward.

Without being asked, the flight attendant passed him a small wrapped package. In it were the tools of his trade; a 9mm Luger complete with shoulder rig—a gun he affectionately called Wilhelmina—and a six-inch, pencil-thin stiletto in a chamois forearm sheath.

The skyway leaked. Through the cracks, he could see gray and drizzle.

That's all right, he thought, *fits my mood.*

He went through the VIP section of customs on his credentials. He rarely traveled as Nick Carter, but he enjoyed it when he did. It was faster.

"Mr. Carter?"

She was pretty, blond, and even the little blue uniform couldn't hide her figure. A French designer would have had a nervous breakdown when he saw what curves could do to a uniform.

"Christine?"

"Yes, sir."

She handed him an envelope. Carter ripped it open. It was a note apologizing for the inconvenience and asking him to please report before going to his hotel.

Carter looked up. "I don't have a hotel and I don't know where to report."

It was obvious from her big-eyed look that he wasn't showing enough team spirit.

"It's about an hour away, sir, in North Kensington."

"Grand. Do I grab a cab?"

"I have a car outside, sir. I'll drive you over."

She turned without another word and led the way out of the terminal and across a puddled parking lot. The uniform didn't hide a bit of the movement.

"How long has it been raining?"

"Five days now."

She was actually cheerful about it.

The car was a new Land-Rover. Carter threw his bags in the back and climbed in the passenger side.

"Who do you work for?" he asked.

"MI5."

"What do you do?"

"Drive."

The engine roared to life and drive she did. By the time they hit the gate of the parking lot, Carter was wildly groping for the seat belt.

"Do you always drive like this?" he asked.

"Oh, yes."

"Is it an hour, *your* drive time, to North Kensington?"

"Yes."

"Tell you what. Let's make it an hour and twenty minutes, okay?"

She slowed down. "Terribly sorry."

Carter unscrewed one of the little bottles. "MI5 Main is on King's Road. What's this place?"

"I don't know, sir. I say, what's that?"

"Breakfast," Carter growled.

He finished the bottle and went to sleep. He was positive it was two seconds later when she shook him awake.

"We're here, sir. The tailor shop down the stoop."

"Jolly good." Carter rubbed his eyes and grabbed his bag. "By the way . . ."

"Yes, sir?"

"What do you do after you drive?"

"I go home . . . to my husband." She took off the instant the door closed.

Carter headed across the street. The unrelenting rain fell in sheets and ran like a river into the gutter. He went down the stoop and through a door with ANDREW CUS-TOM TAILORING on its frosted pane.

The bell brought a graying man, about fifty, in a sagging suit that didn't advertise the quality of his work.

"Yes, sir, can I help you, sir?"

Carter held open his wallet, held it in front of the man's face long enough, and said, "Christine sent me."

"Uh, yes, sir. If you'll just follow me."

The Killmaster did, through a workroom, a storage room, and a locked door. Behind it was a dimly lit hall.

"Last door on your right, sir. They are expecting you."

"Thanks."

Carter hit the door and knocked. At the sound of a cheery "Come in," he did.

It was a small office but large enough to house a desk, a round conference table, several easy chairs, a rolling tea cart, and the cream of British intelligence.

Carter dropped his bag and met eyes. There was Jonathan Hart-Davis, a major string puller from MI6, Ernie Nevers from the Home Office, Claude Dakin, Special Branch, and, last but not least, Owen Hamilton, who practically ran MI5.

"Gentlemen," Carter said, "I think we have a quorum."

The laughter was general and friendly. Carter knew them all and had worked with each of them at one time or another. He shook hands all around and took an indicated chair.

Someone shoved a cup of coffee in his hand, and Commander Hamilton took the floor.

"Sorry you missed your man in South America, Carter. We got a copy of your report from Washington last night."

Carter dropped his eyes and dumped the last bottle of Chivas from the plane into the coffee. "It was a plant or pawn. I don't think Abu El Adwan has been in South America for two, maybe three years. I think I was sucked in because I was getting too close to him in Europe."

Commander Hamilton passed a match over his pipe and sucked hard until it was going. "We're sure of it."

Carter's head jerked up and his eyes, less droopy now, flashed alert, centering on Owen Hamilton. "How are you sure of it?"

The commander had been sitting. Now he stood, moved to the wall, and pulled down a map of North Africa.

"There is an oasis, here in the Libyan desert, called Fasba. El Adwan was spotted there two days ago by one of Jonathan's MI6 people. He's in place for a meet. Yesterday morning, your people, Nick, picked up a transmission out of Tripoli, okaying a meeting in Tunisia between someone in Tunisia and El Adwan in four days.''

''With whom?'' Carter asked, turning to the MI6 man, Hart-Davis.

He got a shrug in return. "Sorry, Nick, don't know the answer to that one. It could be the Russians . . . money, arms."

Carter sipped his coffee. "It's my understanding that El Adwan was getting too radical even for the Russians."

"Ours as well," Hamilton said, nodding. "But who he's meeting is beside the point. The point is, if he's on the ground, we figured you deserved the shot at him . . . if you want it.''

"You bet your ass I do."

And Carter meant it.

Abu El Adwan was insane. Besides being a psychopath, he loved the glory his terrorism engendered. He loved to kill; one or a hundred, it didn't matter. But even better, he loved the notoriety that killing gave him.

With Carter's words, the room fell silent. All eyes were on him.

Even Owen Hamilton himself stood, puffing his pipe, his eyes meeting Carter's.

"What is it?"

Jonathan Hart-Davis picked it up. "In the past year, Nick, I've lost two good MI6 men going after this bloody bastard. Not only that, two more of my men had a shot at him and missed. The man moves around like a will-o'-the-wisp and blends in like a chameleon. He never uses the same group twice for his attacks, and even the ones he uses don't know anything about him."

"In short," Ernie Nevers from the Home Office said, "there's not a bloody soul in the world who knows what the bugger looks like . . . except one."

Carter furrowed his brow, concentrated, and then remembered: "Ravelle Dressler."

"That's right," Nevers replied. "Do you remember the story?"

"Some of it, not all."

What he did remember was a brilliant, two-man kill, all executed within an hour of each other a year before in London.

Zev Rosenbaum, a prominent London businessman and a frequent fund raiser for Israeli and Zionist causes, owned an apartment in the Mayfair section of London. Knowing that he was a target, Rosenbaum had practically made his apartment a fortress with elaborate security devices.

Ali Hassain was a Palestinian and a journalist. He was considered a specialist on the Middle East. As a full-time columnist for the London *Times* and a frequent guest on the BBC, plus a regular weekly Wednesday-morning radio program, his views were listened to. The odd thing about Hassain was that he advocated a peaceful solution to the Palestinian problem: he suggested recognizing Israel. This made him a marked man.

Both men shared one major flaw: in their personal lives they tended to be creatures of habit.

Rosenbaum arose each morning at 6:00. For fifteen minutes he exercised, and then entered his bath at 6:15, where he took his morning shower. His routine never varied.

Every Wednesday morning of the year, Ali Hassain left his apartment in Bayswater near Hyde Park at 6:40 to drive to the BBC for his radio show. A driver always picked him up on Wednesday mornings in a car from the BBC motor pool.

On the fateful morning, Zev Rosenbaum stepped into his shower at 6:15, turned it on, and was electrocuted. At 6:41, Ali Hassain stepped into the BBC car, and ten pounds of plastique explosives disintegrated it, instantly killing him and the driver.

At 7:00 sharp, the telephone rang in the flat of Ravelle Dressler. Normally at that hour she would still be in bed, sleeping soundly. She rarely awakened before noon. On this particular morning, violent stomach cramps had awakened her at 6:30. It was later learned that the fillet of sole she had eaten the previous evening at Burdoines restaurant was slightly contaminated.

The touch of food poisoning that had awakened her and drawn her into the kitchen—three rooms from her bedroom—in search of a remedy had saved her life.

At 7:00 her telephone rang. Normally, of course, she would have answered it in her bedroom. She picked up the extension in the kitchen.

"Yes?"

"Good morning, darling."

"Good morning, Rahib. Will you be back today?"

Rahib Salubar was the lady's current lover, and had been for the last three months. The previous evening, he had left the apartment on business, saying he would be back in two or three days' time.

Ravelle Dressler never got an answer to her question. The words had scarcely left her lips when a bomb exploded in the base of the bedroom telephone, demolishing the room and starting a fire.

One hour later, the newsroom of *The Times* received a call. The voice on the phone claimed credit for the deaths of Zev Rosenbaum and Ali Hassain, and identified himself as the voice of worldwide revolution, Abu El Adwan.

It was many hours later that the link was established. El Adwan, posing as a Turkish businessman named Rahib Salubar, had wormed his way into the confidence of Ravelle Dressler. He moved into her Mayfair apartment and became her lover. For three months he rarely went out. When he did, it was to observe Ali Hassain.

The time he spent in her flat he used to break through the rear of one of the woman's closets and literally build himself a passageway between the walls to a similar closet in the flat of Zev Rosenbaum.

On the Tuesday evening before the Wednesday of the assassinations, he rigged the shower for Rosenbaum's death. He then broke into the BBC garage and planted the remote control bomb that would eventually destroy Ali Hassain.

The bomb in Ravelle Dressler's telephone had been installed for days. It, too, was remote-controlled and voice-activated.

The Dressler woman needed to be killed because of her intimacy over such a long period of time. She could identify him. And she was probably the only person in the world who could.

Ernie Nevers was speaking again. "Of course, we implicated Mrs. Dressler even though we knew she had been duped. That has been hanging over her head all this time, as well as the fear that El Adwan would return and finish the job."

Carter stubbed out his cigarette and groaned. "What you're saying is that you and Washington want no slipups this time. You want an eyeball identification of El Adwan."

"That's right," Commander Hamilton replied. "We've

contacted Mrs. Dressler, but we haven't given her all the details."

"You mean you want me to do it?" Carter growled.

"Exactly," Hamilton replied. "And convince her that it would be in her best interests to help us. You have a date tonight, Nick. I do hope you have proper evening wear with you. The woman only goes to the best of places."

TWO

The long black limousine glided almost silently past the main gate of the Mitsubishi shipbuilding plant in Nagasaki. Beyond the gates, even at this late hour, workers swarmed over the hulks of the biggest movable objects ever built by man: supertankers.

Beyond the main gate, the car turned down a narrow street and approached an alternate yard. It was completely obscured by a twenty-foot-high chain link fence backed by boards, with the boards in turn backed by canvas tarpaulins so no inquisitive soul on the outside could monitor the construction on the inside.

There was a single gate. Above it was a logo of the world spouting oil derricks and crisscrossed with hundreds of heavy black lines. Beneath the logo were the

13

words ST. JAMES LINES and THOR PROJECT. Directly under this, in big letters, was CONSTRUCTION BY NAKIMOTO LTD.

At the first sighting of the car, the two diminutive Japanese guards swung the gate wide. Though they couldn't see through the smoky gray windows, they stood back and saluted as the limousine passed through. The gates closed the moment it had cleared.

Before the car lay two enormous pods. On the pods, like two supine skyscrapers, were the hulls of two supertankers that dwarfed others being built not too far away in the regular Mitsubishi plants. Those in the other yards were mere 250,000-tonners, in one case a 500,000-tonner.

The two ships under construction here on the St. James Lines pods were one-million-tonners. Each of them, when completed, would be a quarter of a mile long, a hundred yards wide, and would draw more than 115 feet of water when launched. They would be sixteen stories high at the tip of their superstructure, and would cost one billion dollars each at completion.

As the car rolled up a steep ramp and then up another, the rear window rolled down silently and a face appeared.

The man was heavyset, with a finger of neatly trimmed gray hair around an otherwise bald head. His gray suit was of the finest quality without being ostentatious, and he wore a subdued, blue-striped regimental tie.

The seamed face was immobile, but the blue eyes flashed a diamondlike fire as he gazed down at the two steel behemoths, *Thor I* and *Thor II*. One was practically completed, the other only a shell.

The man was Hannibal St. James. He was seventy-four years old and looked every day of it. He had started life as Theo Stenopoles, the son of a shipwright in his native Greece. In 1940, he had fled the Nazi surge into his native country, taking with him a goodly sum of American money intended for the resistance movement. He had made his way to neutral South America, where he invested wisely and worked hard.

The war was profitable for young Theo. By the time it ended, he was a comparatively rich man.

But not rich enough by far.

He returned to Greece, and in a short time became a black-market kingpin. This proved even more lucrative, and Stenopoles looked for safe investments that would grow. He was a man who always had a vision of progress and growth. He could see that, in time, the world's need for oil would increase, as would the need to transport that oil.

Through bribery, intimidation, and clever financial maneuvering, Stenopoles cornered a large segment of the oil export business from small Third World countries before the rulers of those countries realized the worth of their oil.

Thus Octagon Petroleum was born. Soon after, oil brokerage houses all over the world emerged bearing the Octagon logo. This was when Theo Stenopoles began looking around for a fleet of ships to buy.

He didn't have to look far, nor did he have to buy.

Jeffrey St. James had spent his entire life building up the St. James Lines. At the peak of his success, at age fifty-six, Jeffrey St. James died. Childless, he left everything to his wife, Clarissa.

Clarissa was a charming, not overly intelligent woman who had brought nearly as much money to the marriage as Jeffrey St. James would eventually make.

When Jeffrey died, Clarissa was becalmed in the sea
of life. She had lost the husband who had cared for her
and pampered her, and she was swiftly losing the beauty
that had once made up for her lack of brains.

Theo Stenopoles saved the day. He married the aging
Clarissa and took over her money and her name. He
added Hannibal to the St. James, and became a British
citizen.

For ten years, Hannibal was a faithful husband. This
was easy for him; sex sapped the energy he needed to
make money. Clarissa demanded nothing but clothes,
jewels, servants to pamper her, and advisors to manage
her money.

Hannibal St. James provided all of these in abundance,
with the stipulation that Clarissa leave him alone. This
she did right up until the night she died in a boating
accident off the south coast of France.

Clarissa's death was providential. It gave Hannibal
complete control and allowed him to tell her bankers,
advisors, and solicitors to go to hell. He expanded his
empire, investing in Japanese industry, gold, and Califor-
nia land. He also made heavy investments in the new
rage that was sweeping oil shipping: supertankers.

At the height of the world's oil shortage in the 1970s,
St. James had another vision. His supertankers were making a fortune. Why not build two *super*-supertankers? He
would build two ships that would make the current
monsters seem like canoes by comparison.

He called it the Thor Project.

The international banking world considered the project
crazy and unworkable. They were convinced that if anything went wrong, it could bankrupt both of St. James's
companies.

Hannibal St. James had never been wrong in the past, and he was convinced that he wasn't wrong now. With *Thor I* and *Thor II,* he could so control pricing that he could undercut other lines and scuttle them. Eventually he could buy them up and control the movement of the world's oil.

He told the bankers to go to hell, and underwrote the entire project with his personal fortune.

However, for the first time in his life, Hannibal St. James had made a mistake. The doomsayers had proved correct. Because of falling inflation and the world oil glut, petroleum prices took a nosedive. Suddenly there was no need for supertankers, least of all supertankers of the one-million-ton class.

St. James saw the handwriting on the wail. He stopped work on *Thor II*, and shifted all the men and materials of Nakimoto Ltd. to *Thor I*. Now it was imperative that the huge ship have her maiden voyage as soon as possible. If she didn't, Hannibal St. James might very well spend his twilight years on the dole.

Sitting in the limousine now, staring down at the nearly completed ship, St. James contemplated the enormity of the plan he had put into motion nearly one year before. Its end result would be one of the world's biggest disasters.

But St. James could give a damn about the world. His only interest was in saving his companies.

As Hannibal St. James contemplated the giant steel hulk of his only folly, the man who sat beside him contemplated St. James.

His name was Oliver Estes, a dapper, diminutive man of sixty-four, with sharp features that were not softened by his small goatee and mustache. His dark eyes, behind gold-rimmed spectacles, had a way of focusing on an object until his brain had assimilated every particle of that object.

Oliver Estes was the chief comptroller of the huge Octagon conglomerate, and in all things he mirrored his employer's thinking.

In the whole world, only Estes knew where the bodies were buried. But he would never tell. He couldn't. Even if he was alive, he was one of the bodies. St. James owned him.

Years before, Estes had been a lowly accountant with Octagon. But he was a brilliant one. He managed to embezzle nearly five million dollars from the company coffers. Only the old man himself had discovered the loss. To Estes's surprise, instead of being fired and jailed, St. James had elevated him to the second-most-exalted position in the company.

In the years since, he had become the instrument by which St. James destroyed anything—and anyone—in his way. He had bribed heads of state, ruined the economy of many a small nation, and ordered the assassination of more men than he could remember.

And soon he would again play messenger, this time for the most heinous act St. James had ever conceived. But, like his employer, Oliver Estes thought nothing of it. In fact, a great deal of the plan was his own conception.

"Hannibal, they're coming."

St. James turned in the seat in time to see three men emerge from the shadows and approach the car. The first of the three was small, slightly stooped, and walked with a slight limp. He was Akiri Nakimoto, head of Nakimoto Ltd., one of the largest shipbuilding concerns in the world. The two men trailing him were his sons.

He opened the door and bowed slightly.

"Akiri-san," St. James said. "It is good of you to meet me on such short notice."

"It is my honor."

"Please, get in . . . sit!"

The old Japanese took the jump seat across from St. James, while Estes closed and locked the door. Nakimoto's two sons moved back, lit cigarettes, and eyed the windows their eyes couldn't penetrate.

"Will you meet the deadline?" St. James asked, coming immediately to the point, his tone brusque.

The old Japanese nodded. "Definitely. In fact we should finish one, perhaps two days ahead of schedule."

"Excellent, excellent," St. James said, his skin stretching taut over his gaunt features in a non-smile. "And your sons have followed my orders precisely?"

Nakimoto swallowed audibly and his narrow eyes darted between the two men. He seemed to have trouble formulating a reply. When at last he spoke, his usually flawless English was tinged with an accent.

"Precisely, yes. Only a very few of our people, and those we trust implicitly, have any knowledge of the final materials."

"Then why," Estes asked, "are our contacts at Lloyd's in London so positive that they have sent an investigator?"

Nakimoto began to sweat visibly. "If your insurer is doing an investigation, I am sure it is only fragmentary, from the outside. There are no English or Americans on the work crew. Every person who has handled the construction materials, or worked on the ship itself, is Japanese."

"For God's sake, you old fool," St. James barked, "don't you think Lloyd's is capable of hiring a Japanese investigator to find out the quality of the *Thor I*?"

"Yes, yes, I suppose—"

"Suppose nothing," Estes said, interrupting the other man. "Lloyd's has somehow learned of the lower grade of steel in the storage tanks. They have also learned that the backup radar system has not been installed. I have managed to placate them and cover up these shortages. But they must receive no more inside information."

"Also," St. James said, chiming in, "we received a copy of the order invoice for a backup computer system. We canceled it."

Nakimoto's eyes grew wide with shock and the hands in his lap began to shake. "But that is madness. Should the primary system be disabled for any reason, there would be no way to monitor shift and expansion in the tanks without the backup system!"

St. James leaned forward and gently rested his hand on the Japanese man's knee. "Akiri-san, your job is to build the ship. My request is that you build it to my specifications. You will do that, won't you?"

Again a long swallow, and then a nod. Nakimoto was building a sailing disaster and he knew it. With inferior materials and unskilled labor, he had cut over ninety million dollars from the building costs.

He hated what he was doing, but he would do it. Like Oliver Estes, Akiri Nakimoto was owned by Hannibal St. James.

"And, Mr. Nakimoto," Estes said, "the *Thor I* leaves Japan in three weeks. I want no more information going to London in that time. Go over your list of workmen again."

"But what if I find a suspect?"

"My chauffeur's name is Horst Layman," St. James

replied. "Mr. Estes and I are leaving tonight. Horst will remain. Here is a number where he can be reached. When you learn the identity of the informer, call him. He will handle it."

Nakimoto pocketed the slip of paper and shuddered. He bowed once more and left the car to walk on, supported by his sons.

The door had barely closed behind him when the limousine was in motion.

"What do you think he will do," Estes asked, "when he learns what has happened?"

"Hopefully," St. James replied, "he will kill himself. After all, it is the Japanese way."

THREE

It was the kind of situation Carter hated. Since her affair with El Adwan, Ravelle Dressler had obviously feared for her life every moment. If that were not bad enough, the British authorities had held her complicity with the terrorist as a sword over her head.

Asking her to cooperate was a form of double blackmail that turned the Killmaster's stomach. But he knew it was a necessary evil. The worst part of it was the fact that it was Carter who had to do the convincing.

Good evening, Mrs. Dressler. My name is Carter. I would like you to give up your creature comforts, strike out into the desert, and put your ass on the line while I waltz you up to a man who would desperately like to see you dead!

22

Simple.

The cab eased to a halt across from the building housing Ravelle Dressler's flat. Carter paid the driver, and checked his watch.

He was twenty minutes early.

Good, he thought, and spotted a pub a few doors down. *Gratification.*

"Good evening, what'll it be?"

"Chivas. Better make that a double."

"Bad day, eh?"

"Worse night."

"Right."

The scotch helped. It burned all the way down and mellowed as it settled.

Carter walked out of the pub and crossed the street. Everything about the building was posh, including the Italian marble foyer and the doorman in the middle of it.

"May I help you, sir?"

"Dressler."

"That will be Five-A, sir. Shall I ring you up?"

"No need. I'm expected."

"Right you are, sir. Lifts are there to your right."

There were only two apartments to a floor. Hers was on the left. Carter knocked, and the door opened at once, as if she had been standing behind it.

She probably was, Carter thought, forcing a smile.

"Good evening, Mrs. Dressler, I am—"

"The American, I know."

She didn't invite him in, but let her eyes examine his face and then float down over his tuxedo-clad form.

Carter countered the examination with one of his own.

She was an older woman, naturally; voluptuous in a strapless, garnet red lace-over-satin dress. An opera length double strand of pearls accented the thrust of her breasts

and added to the effect of her height. She was nearly as
tall as Carter.

Her hair was glossy black, worn sleek and shining like
a mirror, drawn into an elaborate knot at the nape of her
neck. There were no bags under her eyes, and the brows
above them had been plucked to an elegant arch. She
had tiny lines from her patrician nose to her thin, artfully
painted lips.

Carter only glanced at the lines, but she caught him
at it. She lifted her hand, the wedding finger laden with
an enormous baroque pearl and diamond ring, and
touched one of the lines.

"I laugh too much," she said, her proper English only
slightly tainted with her native Turkish accent.

"That's good," Carter said. "There's not enough laughter in the world."

The words seemed to relax her. She smiled, and her
face glinted with the beauty that she once possessed,
before the years had crept over her, before she had the
eye-lift responsible for the smooth, tight look across the
upper part of her face.

Carter wondered why she hadn't gone the whole route
and had the laugh lines softened. Then he realized that
would have made it necessary for her to abandon the
sleek hairstyle to hide the scars.

"Shall we go?" he asked.

"Oh, sorry, I haven't asked you in. How stupid of me
. . . not very hospitable."

"That's probably because you're nervous."

"You're too polite, Mr. . . . ?"

"Carter. Nick Carter."

"Of course."

She caught up a short jacket of garnet velvet and a

glittering evening bag. "I've made reservations at Colombe. Do you know it?"

"I'm afraid not," Carter replied.

"It's new."

She spoke only once in the cab. "Why have they sent you?"

"To identify someone."

"Rahib?"

"That's right. Except that his real name is Abu El Adwan."

She shuddered, and then managed a smile and a sighing quip. "Good old Ravelle, the terrorist's moll. What a bloody fool I was."

The vast, newly decorated dining room was filled with flowers and the whisper of music from a good dance band. Most of the peach-covered tables were occupied. Several couples were dancing. All sound was subdued, blending into the music. Waiters moved about quickly, unobtrusively.

The maître d' escorted them to their table. It stood out from the wall, which was latticed and on which fresh flowers had been placed thickly enough to cover it.

They certainly don't stop at expense, Carter thought, knowing that, by morning, the fragile blossoms would be dead. They would have to be replaced every afternoon, not long before the diners began to arrive.

A steward came with the wine list. He presented it to Carter, who looked across the table inquiringly.

"God, no." Ravelle smiled. "Scotch, a double."

"Make it two," Carter said.

The steward left so quickly that Carter was surprised he was gone. "No waste of time," he said, and grinned.

"They are paid to be quick," she replied, her eyes

narrowing as they met Carter's. "You're different."

"Than who?"

"The others who have been browbeating me for the past year, the ones who come around with their rude questions and keep shoving photos under my nose."

"What kind of man was he?"

"Rahib? . . . Or, as you call him, El Adwan? I'm sure you've read my statement."

Carter nodded. "But I'd like to hear it directly."

"He was charming, very handsome, and he had a beautiful body. Also, he was quite a good lover. Are you a good lover, Nick Carter?"

"I've had no complaints."

"Good," she said, smiling a real smile for a change.

They dawdled over dinner for an hour and then, between brandies, danced. She was a lithe, smooth dancer. Her body didn't really move, it glided. Carter remembered that she had been a professional dancer in Istanbul when she met her husband.

He asked.

"It's not much of a story. My parents were financially comfortable. I was well educated. They died in a plane crash when I was eighteen. In two years, I managed to go through every penny of my inheritance. I had no skills, but I was fairly attractive and I had a quite striking body. I could be a prostitute or a belly dancer. I chose the latter. I danced for five years. Then, one night, I met Dressler. He became infatuated and we married. We were married for twenty years. There was a great deal of money. We were society. We had many friends. Then it happened."

"What happened?" Carter asked, already knowing.

"He fell in love. Sixty-one years old, and he fell in love with a girl young enough to be his granddaughter. Eighteen years old . . . *eighteen!*"

"Did she look like you when you were eighteen?"

"The spitting image. But he was generous. He settled a million pounds on me. He admitted I'd been a good wife, but said that this great new 'love' rendered him helpless."

"Where is he now?"

"Dead. He made some terrible investments and lost every sou. He shot himself, and his great 'love' took to the streets of Soho. Ironic, isn't it?"

"Very."

"Even more ironic is the fact that we had the same money manager, a chap named Oliver Estes. Dressler went broke on Oliver's advice, and I profited. It was at one of Oliver's parties that I met Rahib . . . excuse me, El Adwan." She shook her head. "I can't imagine him having such a name. It seems so overly dramatic."

Carter instantly came alert. "That wasn't in your report to the Home Office. In the report you said you met him by chance in a nightclub."

Her face suddenly glowed pink. "Well, in polite society you don't exactly meet a perfect stranger at a posh party, know him for fifteen minutes, and be romping with him in one of your host's upstairs bedrooms!"

"But you did?"

Her face gained a deeper flush. "Yes, frankly, I couldn't resist. And then, about a month later, I met him at a private gambling club. I hardly recognized him."

"Why?"

"At the party, he had a black beard and I could have sworn his eyes were blue. At the club, he was clean-shaven and his eyes were dark brown."

The man is a chameleon. He can change to blend into any situation. . . .

"This Estes chap . . . how well did he know El Adwan?"

"Hardly at all, I think," she said with a shrug. "I had the feeling that Rahib arrived with a little blond twit who was a professional bed partner for visiting VIPs."

Carter made a mental note of this, and signaled for the check.

In the cab, he explained the situation. He was scarcely halfway through when her complexion lightened several degrees.

"Are you mad?" she cried. "If I got close enough to identify him, I'd be putting my neck on the chopping block!"

"Not really," Carter replied calmly. "You'll go into Tunis on a forged passport. You'll be gowned and veiled as a Moslem woman. You speak perfect Arabic, and I'll be watching over you every second of the time."

Silence, a lot of it.

"I can't do it," she said at last. "I've lived in too much fear of him for a year. I would break—I know I would."

"You would be safe. All I need is a positive identification. Once you've done that, your part is over."

Suddenly she whirled in the seat. "What happens after I identify him?"

Carter weighed her mood, the look in her dark eyes, and the tenseness in her body.

He decided to go for broke.

"I'm going to kill him."

Her first words inside the apartment were, "I'll get comfortable."

Carter knew it was only the prelude, but he didn't mind. In the last three hours, Ravelle Dressler had grown on him. He knew she was thinking, thinking hard, and if his hanging around until ham-and-eggs time would help her come up with an answer, so be it.

He found snifters and a bottle of good cognac at the bar. By the time he poured, she had returned and cuddled up on one of the sofas.

"Cheers."

"Cheers," she replied, naked except for a midnight blue lace peignoir. She sipped from the glass and lowered it slowly from her lips. "I'll bet you're beautiful naked."

"Men aren't beautiful," Carter said, moving in beside her.

"It depends on who is doing the looking."

She smiled at him, slowly, the laugh lines cutting deep, and he smiled back. Somehow the glasses found the coffee table without spilling. Her lips came up to meet his, and they kissed with a fierceness that fueled the desire in both their bodies.

His tongue circled and probed, riding along her teeth, and then met her tongue. She moaned deep in her throat and her body arched, telling him what he already knew.

"Put your arms up," he murmured.

She did, and her breasts peaked up into two hard points beneath the lacy gown. They rose and fell with her breathing as he grasped the hem of the gown and inverted it. Then he peeled it up, over her head until she was naked.

"*You* are beautiful," he said.

"You . . . you don't have to do this, you know."

"This is pleasure, not business," he whispered.

He slid both palms down around her neck, her collarbone, then outward to the top curves of her breasts. Her lips quivered and her own hands went to work on his clothing. He continued with his hands to the soft lower swells of her breasts, carefully avoiding the nipples, which stood out like twin jewels in identical mounts.

His mouth watered for them, but still he touched only the tender skin surrounding them. Her breasts were heavy, swollen with desire, and they filled his palms.

"Stand up," she ordered breathily.

He stood, and moved his hands around to her back as she removed his clothes. When she finished, he turned her back to his front and pulled her tautly against him.

"I can feel you," she gasped.

"How can you not?" he whispered, as his hands moved into the hollow above her navel and his lips kissed her naked shoulder.

"My nipples," she begged, "touch my nipples!"

He did, and the effect was electric. Suddenly they were sinking as one to the floor, her distended nipples drilling into his palms.

She lay back on the soft carpet, her hair spreading outward like a dark halo. As Carter moved over her, she reached up and caressed his face. He raised his head and looked down at her. Her eyes slowly opened and closed, telling him of her need. His eyes darted back and forth over her voluptuous form, and his body trembled with excitement.

Suddenly she pulled herself up toward him, her lips hungrily covering his with a warm, damp pressure. Carter could feel the tip of her tongue flicking back and forth. He opened his mouth wide and slid his lips over hers, stiffening his tongue and pushing it inside. Her tongue curled around his as one of his hands moved between her thighs, his fingers working in the moistness they found there.

"Oh, God, hurry . . . now!" she gasped. "I'm ready for you!"

Carter bent over her and trailed his lips down her silky skin from her throat to one of her breasts. The tip of his tongue flicked across the bud of her nipple, and a soft cry came from her lips. He let the nipple slide into his mouth and gently sucked on it.

Her breath hissed out through her teeth as his lips and tongue slowly moved down her stomach until his chin brushed her inner thighs. He lifted his head, letting his moist breath caress the lower part of her stomach. He put his hands on her thighs and held her fast as he stimulated her with hard, quick touches of his tongue.

"Please, please!" she pleaded, arching her lower body toward him and flinging her head from side to side.

Carter moved up over her. Her face was flushed and drawn with passion. Her lips were pulled back from her teeth. They were moist and crimson, and her eyes flashed with anticipation.

Her hand moved downward, found him, and guided him inside her. He pulled her hard against him until the breath was forced from her lungs in a scream of fulfillment.

A wave of sensation roared through his body as they were joined. She wiggled her hips as she arched her back to take him, deeper and deeper.

Carter gripped her waist and rocked his hips, slowly floating on a blissful cloud of sensual enjoyment as he felt her warmth engulf him.

"Good," she whispered, matching him movement for movement, "so good."

They moved together, increasing the pace of their lovemaking until it became the fury of climax.

Slowly he slid to her side. "You're a wildcat," he said huskily.

"And you're an animal," she purred. "I wouldn't miss it."

"What?"

"North Africa," she replied. "When do we leave?"

"Tomorrow night." Her lips kissed their way down over his chest and stomach until they found him. "If I'm alive."

FOUR

His name was Ishu Tanaki. He had been trained in England and the United States as a maritime engineer specializing in seagoing salvage. He was fluent in Japanese, English, and Mandarin Chinese. For the past five years he had worked for Lloyd's as an investigator. In that time, he had saved them millions in fraudulent claims in salvage. Now he was on to something that would make all his earlier jobs insignificant by comparison.

The previous afternoon, the International Maritime Commission representatives had gone over the *Thor I* with a fine-tooth comb. They had barely left the ship, pronouncing her seaworthy and meeting all standards, when an elite crew of dismantlers had come aboard.

Secretly, beyond the eyes of the workmen putting the finishing touches on the huge tanker, this crew had dismantled the backup radar system, the communication system, and the ever-so-important emergency backup system that controlled the flow and seepage in the gigantic tanks that would soon hold several hundred thousand barrels of crude oil.

Tanaki, as a stress expert, had the run of the ship. His job was to make sure that the huge plates of steel that made up the undersea hull of the tanker and the plates of the tanks inside the hull would give and take with the pounding of the sea.

Tanaki had seen and photographed the dismantling of the ship's backup navigation and safety systems. When that information was passed along to his co-worker from Lloyd's, Carolyn Reed, then relayed to London, a full-scale surprise investigation could be ordered and the sailing date of the *Thor I* scuttled.

Tanaki was a thorough man. He wanted one more nail in the coffin of St. James Lines and Nakimoto Ltd. For the past week he had spent his lunch hour deep in the bowels of the *Thor I* with a portable spectomagraph, an instrument that tested the grade, durability, strength, and thickness of steel. In that time, he had worked from the bow amidships and from the stern amidships, on the outer and inner hull. Now, on this last day before handing over his figures to Carolyn Reed to run through her magic computer, he was testing the tanks themselves.

Like a shadow he moved through the deepest compartments of the ship, the huge boiler and engine rooms housing the giant dynoturbines, among the forty-foot-high banks and generators and turbo-alternators, inside the

air-conditioning and ventilating plants—all the vital or-
gans that made the *Thor I* a self-contained city at sea.

By the time he was ready to return to the regular job
that had brought him aboard the *Thor I*, he had more
than enough data to give to Carolyn Reed. And even
without the hundreds of calibrations and equations her
computer would make, Ishu Tanaki knew that the *Thor
I* at sea would be a floating time bomb.

In a small hotel just across from the huge Hamacho
shopping arcade, Horst Layman waited and drank. He
would have liked to take a little time out and gone down
to the port, to one of the hostess bars, to find a woman.
But he had no idea when the call would come. Hannibal
St. James's orders had been to sit and wait. So Horst
Layman sat and waited. He always followed Mr. St.
James's orders to the letter, no matter what they were.
Like Oliver Estes and so many others, Horst Layman
was owned, body and soul, by Hannibal St. James.

He was a grotesquely large man, with blunt features,
blue eyes that seemed opaque, and brush-cut gray hair.
He seemed to have no neck, so his massive head sat
directly on his equally gargantuan shoulders.

Layman had once been a bouncer in a Berlin nightclub,
with ambitions of becoming the heavyweight boxing
champion of the world. Two things thwarted his ambitions. One was the fact that his speed never matched his
massive strength. The other was his propensity for drink
and what it caused him to do . . . kill people, usually
women, most often prostitutes.

For years, his habit went undetected. When he was
finally caught, it was not by the police but by Hannibal
St. James. Rather than turn him over to the authorities,

St. James hired him. It was the perfect solution for Horst Layman. He could go on with his odd life, as long as a certain percentage of the people he terminated were the enemies of Hannibal St. James.

The bottle came to his lips and the last of its contents disappeared, a portion of the liquid dribbling over his chin. It was the second bottle he had consumed in as many hours, and he seemed surprised that it was gone.

In disgust, he threw it aside and reached for the telephone to order another. Just as the beefy fingers curled around the instrument, it rang.

"Yes?"

"Mister Layman?"

"Yes." He recognized the tenor voice and accented English of one of Akiri Nakimoto's two sons.

"His name is Ishu Tanaki. He is on the second shift, working tonight. His shift ends at midnight. He has a small flat at Eight Shimbasi, in the Okon section. He drives a late-model Toyota, green, license 484-10-991. Do you need to know anything else?"

"No. You are sure he is the man?"

"Yes. A check of his locker and an eyewitness to some of his lunchtime activities have confirmed."

"Good."

Horst Layman hung up the phone and lumbered from the room. His movements were steady and his eyes were bright and clear. There was not the slightest indication that he had just consumed two fifths of scotch whiskey.

Ishu Tanaki threw the last of his clothing into a soft-sided flight bag and surveyed the room for anything he might have missed. Only his notebook remained. He slipped that into his coat pocket and moved across the room to the phone.

He had tried Carolyn Reed's hotel four times in the half hour since he had left the shipyards, and there had been no answer. This, the fifth time, produced results. The calm, cool voice with the very British accent picked up on the first ring.

"It's me. I've been trying to reach you."

"A conference call with London. I had to take it in the lobby exchange. It seems they are very nervous about our last two reports."

Tanaki chuckled. "They should be. They will be even more nervous after tonight. I'm packing it in. I've got it all."

"You're sure?"

"Positive. Either St. James is planning to never launch the *Thor,* or he's going to scuttle her. I've got positive specs. I'll see you within the hour."

"I'll be packed."

Tanaki hung up and grabbed his bag. He opened the door, took one step into the hall, and was suddenly flying through the air. He hit the far wall, hard, and slipped to the floor, little rockets exploding behind his eyes. When he could focus again, he saw an enormous man close the door and move toward him.

The nearer the man got, the larger he got. Tanaki closed his eyes, strained them, and opened them again in hopes that the mountain of flesh in a dark suit would disappear.

It didn't.

One hand gathered the front of Tanaki's sweater and he was yanked into the air. The powerful fingers of another hand wrapped around his throat.

If Tanaki hadn't gotten the message before, he got it now. The enormous blob with the big head meant to kill him.

The little Japanese lashed out with both feet, burying his toes in the other man's gut. There was a grunt and a wide-eyed stare of surprise from the giant, but nothing more. Tanaki followed the kick with a blast from both palms to the man's ears.

This produced results, a growl of pain and a back-handed blow across the mouth that sent Tanaki back across the room. He lifted himself on one elbow, spitting teeth and snarling.

"Come," the giant said, placidly motioning with a huge hand.

Aside from everything else he'd mastered, Ishu Tanaki was also an expert in martial arts. He came in low, did a flip onto his hands, and aimed a vicious, bone-shattering kick at the other man's jaw.

Only the jaw wasn't there. Nothing was there except air.

Again Tanaki was airborne. But this time he was arrested in mid-flight when the giant grasped his wrists. At the same time, both arms were wrenched up to his shoulder blades. There was a twin cracking sound, and the Japanese knew that both his arms had been broken.

He started to scream, when a hand slapped the sound back down his throat. Then he was up against the wall, blood streaming from his broken nose. Through the misty tears of pain in his eyes, he could see the other man's leering face, his thick lips spread wide over yellowish teeth in an evil grin of sheer delight.

Not only does he plan to kill me, Tanaki thought, *but he plans on getting a great deal of enjoyment out of the act.*

The little Japanese knew then that he had nothing to lose. He reared forward, colliding his forehead with the man's nose. He continued the motion until he could sink his teeth into the side of the giant's throat.

It was futile. The man had no neck, and what Tanaki could reach was pure gristle that not even the strength of his jaws could penetrate.

The hands came up. They curled around Tanaki's throat. Now there was no emotion in the wide, flat face; even the grin was gone.

"Why?" Tanaki managed to gurgle.

It was the last word he spoke.

When the body stopped dancing, Horst Layman dropped it to the floor. He removed his coat and pulled on a pair of surgical gloves.

Then he went through every item in Tanaki's pockets, wallet, briefcase, and flight bag. All the reports, notes, and personal items, he placed in the briefcase.

His car was parked in a narrow alley behind the apartment house. When the bags were in the rear, Layman returned for the body. When it was safely in the trunk, he returned to the tiny apartment and made a last check.

Tanaki himself had left a note for the old *mama-san* who handled the apartments. Layman couldn't read Japanese, but the yen—and the way it and the note were placed on the dresser so they wouldn't be missed—told the story.

Ishu Tanaki had been forced to leave before his time was due. The money and the note explained it all.

Carefully, the big man locked the apartment, slid the key under the thin mat over the tatami floor covering, and returned to his car.

He drove north around Peace Park, and then past the railroad station toward the huge new industrial city outside the old town. When he was in the center of a hundred

belching smokestacks, he turned down a narrow, almost
pitch-dark street, and passed through a large gate. Normally, these gates would be closed and locked. Tonight
they were open. At a loading dock, he stopped.

There was a sign in both Japanese and English high
above the dock, embedded in the brick wall of the building. It said MISHI STEEL WORKS—A DIVISION OF
NAKIMOTO LTD.

A half hour later, Ishu Tanaki and his personal belong-
ings had become one with the black smoke blasting from
the chimneys above the huge Mishi smelters.

Horst Layman drove north, toward Tokyo, with the
Japanese man's briefcase on the seat beside him.

FIVE

They caught the evening flight from London to Paris. Then it was an AXE safe house, where Carter underwent a skin-darkening process, a change in hairstyle, and the addition of a heavy dark mustache.

No makeup was needed for Ravelle Dressler. Only a slight change in hairstyle and the wardrobe of a devout Moslem woman transformed her into a traditional Arab wife.

They emerged as Monsieur and Madame Kalimendar of Paris, he a professor of African civilizations at the Sorbonne, she his dutiful wife complete in robes and veil.

At eight the next morning, they were on a plane to Rome for a connection to Tunis. Flying time from Rome to Carthage was one hour. They landed at three, and had only a one-hour wait for the connection commuter flight to Medenine.

The plane was an ancient two-prop job left over from another time, and the pilot looked like a teen-ager.

But it flew, and an hour later they were heading it over the Gulf of Gabes and banking south for the approach to the desert town of Medenine.

Ravelle's hand gripped Carter's like a vise when the wheels came down.

"It's only the landing gear."

"I know," she replied. "That wasn't what scared me."

"What then?"

"That."

Carter leaned across her and glanced out the window. For as far as the eye could see there was heat haze and, beneath that, nothing but Sahara sand.

He understood. Somewhere out in that vast nowhere, in two days' time, they would be trying to find the man who would dearly love to see both of them dead.

"Watch your veil," he murmured. "Here we go."

They had the brief impression of mountainlike sand dunes rushing toward them, quickly replaced by the white and tan of buildings.

Then they were down, the undercarriage nuzzling the runway, a couple of camels to their right pausing to look with boredom at the noisy bird invading their tranquility.

Very slowly, the plane rolled to a halt in front of a haphazard collection of sheds.

"What the hell is this?" Ravelle asked.

"The airport," Carter whispered in reply.

"Oh, my God."

"And don't look so surprised. We're old North African hands, remember?"

He took her case and followed her down the gangway. Outside, the heat hit viciously, blurring the outlines of the nearby buildings. Over the concrete shack that seemed to be the control tower, a windsock bellied with wind one instant and went limp the next, only to belly suddenly in the opposite direction.

Carter could now understand the swing-and-sway landing.

Tunisia's small-country status between two larger, politically dissimilar countries—Libya and Algeria—made its government a little spiny about travelers away from the regular tourist coastal areas. The city of Medenine was a good example. Three army officers awaited them in tiny booths with turnstiles marked Customs.

As they filed in, Carter gave Ravelle her case and slipped into the line in front of her. If they asked tricky questions, he wanted her to get the clues to answers from him.

The short line moved slowly between railings. This was due to the fact that all three officers were working one booth. They wore old-fashioned tunics, buttoned up to the throat. Two of them, older and squat, looked as if they were masquerading as officials. The third was younger, fresh-faced, and all business when he took the two passports.

"Monsieur Kalimendar . . . how long will you be staying in Tunisia?" His French was fluent and precise.

"Two, perhaps three weeks," Carter replied.

"And the purpose of your visit?"

"I will be doing some research for a book on Sahara oases and their peoples."

"You were born in Paris . . ."

"That is correct."

His intense eyes swiveled to Ravelle. "But your wife was born in Fez, Morocco," he said in staccato Arabic.

"I have been a naturalized French citizen for ten years," she replied, also in perfect Arabic with only a slight variation in accents.

Back to Carter. "And where will you be staying, monsieur?"

"The Hotel Africa . . . for the time being."

He handed the passports back with the suggestion of a smile. "Enjoy your stay in my country."

"Thank you."

They both made their way to the baggage claim.

"His eyes made my skin crawl," Ravelle whispered.

"All customs people have eyes like that," Carter said, and grabbed their bags from the few that were left. The luggage had already been checked by customs in Tunis.

Outside, there were three cabs. Carter held back until the first in line was taken by another couple. They dived into the second, a four-door Fiat that had probably been ancient the day it was born. The desert did that to both people and machines.

"Hotel Africa."

The driver nodded, grunted, and they fled in a cloud of black smoke.

Carter sat back in the seat, glad of the air that seemed cooler as it rushed through the cab's open windows. Medenine had once been a tiny oasis with a few mud huts and few people. Now it was considered a city, with fifteen thousand souls and a lot of mud huts. But it did have a souk and a mosque. The Hotel Africa was near the entrance to the souk or old city and marketplace. That was why Carter had chosen it. That, and the fact that it advertised modern, Western-style rooms with security locks on all doors.

A modern deadbolt lock on a door might not stop Abu El Adwan, but it might deter him or slow him up for a while.

The hotel was the tallest structure around, five stories. It was painted white and looked cool. A porter carried in their bags. The concierge had dark skin, no smile, and an assessor's eye. He acknowledged the reservation, fourth-floor corner with a private bath.

Carter registered while the passport numbers were entered in the police book, and paid the first night in cash.

"And how long will you be staying, monsieur?"

"A week, perhaps two."

The concierge snapped his fingers and gave the key to a baggage man. "Four-oh-six," he barked, and the little man, bags in hand, hit the stairs. There was a reason for this; no more than two people could fit into the ancient caged elevator.

Carter tipped the baggage man and locked the door behind him.

It was a big room with a balcony. A connecting door was locked and bolted on their side.

Ravelle's first move was to shed the heavy robes and veil. Her next was to dig a bottle of scotch from her bag and fix two drinks. She served him one, looking very provocative in only a bra and pair of brief panties.

Carter had to smile. "You lack proper Moslem modesty."

"It's a myth that those bloody robes are cool. Cheers."

"Cheers."

They drank, and Carter noticed that the smile faded when the glass came away from her lips. In the light from the open doors to the balcony, the fine lines around her eyes were more pronounced. There was a look of resignation in her face. The gaiety of the past two days was gone.

"What now?" she asked.

"I make contact. A merchant in the souk named Harik Sabone is on our side."

She moved to him, her eyebrows at an even greater angle than usual. "You're leaving me alone?"

"Have to. It will only be for an hour, two at the most. You'll be safe. Just lock and bolt the door behind me, and let no one in no matter who they say they are."

"If anyone so much as touches that door, I'll pee my pants."

Carter laughed and brushed her lips with his. "Take a long, cool bath. I'll be back before you know it."

"You couldn't leave me a gun or something, could you?"

"You'd probably shoot yourself. And besides, I don't have one."

Her knuckles went white on the glass. "You don't have a gun?"

"Shh, not so loud. It would have been too risky with customs. That's another reason I have to see Sabone."

He noticed, as he left, that she was refilling her glass with scotch, to the top.

He waited until he heard both locks click in place, and then took the elevator to the lobby. The concierge scarcely looked up from his newspaper, and the porter dozed as Carter passed him and walked into the harsh glare of the late-afternoon sun.

The entrance to the souk was two blocks to his left. He turned right and lit a cigarette as he meandered through the newer part of the town. When he was sure that he wasn't being followed, he worked his way back and entered the almost dim, narrow walkways of the old marketplace.

Once inside the souk, he walked briskly. He only had general directions, but the area wasn't large enough not to cover in a short time. It took only ten minutes to find the shop. The windows were cluttered with carpets, old swords and daggers, brass cookware, and assorted desert brick-a-brac. In arabic and French, the sign read HARIK SABONE, ANTIQUES.

Carter entered a small café across the street and ordered coffee. For another ten minutes he sipped the thick liquid and watched the shop. No customers entered or left, and twice he saw vague movement through the windows.

Satisfied, he paid and moved across the street. After letting his eye catch something in the window, he entered to the tinkling of a small bell above the door.

A tall, fat man in a shabby, three-piece suit sidled through a pair of frayed curtains. He was smiling, but the smile just hung there, as if the man forgot what it was for. His bald head was damp with perspiration, the flesh-rimmed eyes were lusterless, and the corpulent cheeks sagged like the breasts of an overused whore.

"Good afternoon. May I help you?" the man asked in guttural Arabic.

"My French is better than my Arabic," Carter replied.

"Then may I help you in French?"

"You are Monsieur Harik Sabone?"

"I am."

"My name is Kalimendar. I understand you have a fine collection of sixteenth-century Berber hand weapons."

The man's face could be extravagantly mobile. As it was, only an eyebrow was raised and the saggy cheeks jiggled only a second.

"This way, please."

Carter followed him through the curtain and a larger room that obviously served as a storage area. Another curtain led them into a tiny office.

"I can hear the bell easily from here, but there will be few customers. You are prompt."

"We had good flight connections," Carter replied, taking a proffered chair and lighting a cigarette.

"I have fresh coffee brewing."

"Yes, I can smell it."

"Would you like coffee . . . or a drink?"

"Coffee, please."

"A moment."

Sabone wiped two tiny cups with a dust rag and poured coffee that was more like molasses. When the amenities were observed—as they always must be in any Arab country, even if the business is clandestine—Sabone spoke.

"Your man is preparing to come over tomorrow night from Libya."

"Where?" Carter asked.

"Near Dehibat. It's about a hundred miles south of here."

"In the desert?"

"Yes. The actual meeting will take place at an oasis near Dehibat. There are three of them, all secluded. As usual, El Adwan is very cautious. The actual hour of his arrival, and which oasis, will be chosen at the last minute."

"What do you suggest?" Carter asked, struggling with the coffee and finally setting it aside.

"I have already arranged for your transportation, and the contact in Dehibat is in place. He is a camel trader

named Bassam. You will meet him in the Café Sultan in
Dehibat tomorrow evening at the supper hour. By then
he will have the location."

"And my equipment?"

"No. At noon tomorrow, a driver will pick you up at
your hotel. His name is Ami. He will also be your backup
in the kill."

"He is a good man?"

"Very, and can be trusted. He is the brother of my
wife."

Carter leaned forward, stubbing out his cigarette. "Is
there any indication of who El Adwan is meeting?"

"None, but he has been recruiting in Libya, Malta,
and Port Said, Egypt, with the promise of great sums of
money. So we know some kind of special operation is
under way." Here, Sabone paused. "This woman, Ravelle
Dressler?"

"Yes."

"Will she hold up long enough to make the identification?"

Carter shrugged. "She has every reason to want him
dead. I think she will."

Sabone nodded and opened a drawer in the desk. From
it he took a 9mm Beretta and two extra, loaded clips.
He passed them across the desk with a smile.

"The bullets have been indented and dipped."

"Cyanide?"

"Of course. This should get you through the night,
until Ami picks you up tomorrow."

Carter got to his feet. "Is there any chance that El
Adwan has been warned?"

Sabone shrugged. "There is always the chance. For,
being such an elusive character, the man has antennae

everywhere. Also, out of necessity, there are four others besides myself who know you are in Tunisia. There is always the chance."

Carter nodded and slipped the gun into his belt, the extra clips into his jacket pocket. "Your people have taken the pictures of El Adwan and the decoys?"

"Hopefully, Bassam will have them when he meets you."

"Hopefully," Carter said dryly, and left the shop.

He used the same roundabout route in his return to the hotel. At the door of the room, he knocked and identified himself before using his key.

Ravelle was on the bed. She had discarded her underwear and pulled on a light robe, but hadn't bothered to belt it. Her hair was still wet from her bath. She was also very drunk.

Carter said so.

"I know. Angry?"

"Not really," he replied, pulling her gently to her feet. "But you could have waited for me."

"No way," she whispered, her lips and tongue doing marvelous things to one of his ears. "I want you sober."

She wound her arms around his neck and strained close to him until her breasts surged against his chest. Without releasing her, Carter shrugged out of his jacket and unbuttoned his shirt. Then he pushed the robe off her shoulders.

"We should get some food into you."

"Later," she groaned.

He swung her off her feet and settled her onto the bed. Somehow he shed his clothes and eased his body along the smooth length of hers.

From there on, he had a tiger by the tail.

•   •   •

So close to the endless silence of the desert, even at the hour of sunrise, there was the echo of camels' hooves on a distant street coupled with the coughing of an automobile engine.

"Well?" she said.

Every few moments her face was dimly illuminated on the pillow as Carter drew on his cigarette. The last hours had been, to say the least, tumultuous. Ravelle had been possessed of a passion that went beyond pleasure.

Now, exhausted, she lay very still, talking in a manner that was quiet and yet almost compulsive.

"You're shocked?"

"No," Carter replied.

"Most men are, afterward. I am the sort they fight to get, but revile in the morning."

Carter was silent.

"Most men think of their mothers or their sisters or their wives, and hope none of them are secretly like me. It has always been my opinion that the man is a big hypocrite in these matters. Far more so than any woman."

"I'm different."

She sighed. "God knows you are."

He blew smoke toward the ceiling. Her hand came along his body to his face. Very gently, her fingers touched his nose, his lips, his brow—then his shoulder, and down his arm to his hand.

She lifted the cigarette from his fingers, took a deep drag, and crushed it out.

"Will I have to meet him face to face?"

"I hope not. There are three possible destinations. El Adwan will come over along with three decoys. Sabone's people are taking photographs on the other side. With luck, you can make a positive ID from one of those."

"When do we leave?"

"At noon," he said.

"Then we had better get some sleep."

She curled into his arm and put her head on his shoulder. In seconds she was sound asleep, breathing evenly.

Carter was glad she hadn't asked what they would have to do if she couldn't make a positive ID from the pictures.

SIX

The Land-Rover had lost all its paint and seen many miles, but it was sound. So was the quiet, robed driver named Ami. He was prompt to the minute, and by one o'clock they were in the desert.

In a small wadi, he stopped and directed Carter to follow him around the vehicle. He opened a false rear tank so the Killmaster could inspect the equipment.

Inside was a Mannlichter single-action CD-13 sniper rifle. It was fitted with a Startron night scope and a resting tripod.

If the Killmaster could get one clean kill shot in, there would be no need to start a desert war.

If not, the other hardware was available: two Ingram

M-11s with lots of steel-jacketed .380s, and two belts of grenandes.

"Good?"

"Good," Carter said, nodding.

Ami locked up the tank and they climbed back into the Land-Rover. The Arab was definitely a man of very few words.

"What was that all about?" Ravelle asked.

"You don't want to know."

They met and cut around two small caravans, and reached the outskirts of Dehibat just before dusk. Ami found a small wadi, and without asking for aid rigged a tent camp. When he was finished he sidled over to Carter, who was already building a fire.

"I be back, quick. Get horses."

Before he could move away, Ravelle stopped him in clipped Arabic. "Why do we need horses?"

"Horses don't make the sound of an engine in the desert night."

It could have been right out of Kipling, but it didn't amuse Ravelle. She whirled on Carter. "What are the horses for?"

He explained. "We have to get in quiet and out fast. Hopefully, we'll be going over terrain that no vehicle could follow."

"How many horses is he getting?"

Carter looked to Ami, who held up two fingers.

"No way!" she cried.

"You'll be safe here, and I'll leave the Beretta," he said.

"No fucking way!" she shrieked. "You tell him to get *three* horses. I'm not staying out in this damn sand alone, wondering what the hell is going on and if you're ever coming back for me!"

"Ravelle . . ."

She dropped into a lotus position in front of the tent and crossed her arms defiantly under her breasts. If that didn't say it all, the grinding of her teeth did.

"Ami . . ."

"Yes?"

"Three horses."

The Arab gave Carter a look that said *It is a pity you cannot control your woman* and climbed into the Land-Rover.

By the time he returned, Carter had a meal of beans, mutton, and sugar cakes ready. Three saddled dapple gray Arabians—two geldings and a mare—were on lead ropes behind the Land-Rover.

"*Three* horses," Ami grunted as he crouched by the fire and helped himself to the food.

"I can see that," Carter replied.

They ate in silence as the sun slipped down behind the dunes. By the time they had finished and Carter had changed into robes and a burnoose, it was pitch-dark.

"Café Sultan is the first alley to the right off the center round."

"I'll find it," Carter said, carefully folding a sash over the Beretta.

"You ride?"

"No. It's a mile. I'll walk." He moved to Ravelle. "Do me a favor."

"What?"

"Behave yourself."

She glanced toward Ami. "Don't worry—he's not my type."

"That's not what I . . . never mind."

Lifting his robes, Carter side-walked up the wall of

the wadi and headed toward the flickering lights of Dehibat.

There was only one main street, so following it brought
Carter easily to the center of the village. It was near the
supper hour, so there were few people outside. The smell
of food—cooked and uncooked—was heavy in the air.
He spotted the alley and moved into it.

Twice he moved into a darkened doorway to let robed
men pass him. They had the smell of camels about them,
and their dark faces from life under the desert sun were
like apparitions from the *Arabian Nights*.

The Café Sultan was on another, smaller square, with
alleys leading into it. The café itself was a small place
with a hand-lettered sign in Arabic. It had a dirty plate
glass window where a torn velvet portiere hung on a
wooden rod.

Inside, the room was stifling. Acrid cigarette smoke
hung thick under the low ceiling. A few blank-faced men
in from the desert sat sipping mint tea and gnawing food.
There were only two men in Western clothes. One was
young. He sat by the window staring at nothing. With
only one quick sniff, Carter could smell the aura of hash-
ish hovering about his head.

The Killmaster headed for the other. He sat in a rear
corner table, well chosen for its lack of light.

Carter paused by the table. The seated man idly held
his palm before his face, his elbow casually on the scarred
wood. When the man nodded, Carter slid into a chair.

"I am Bassam." He dropped his hand to reveal a snap-
shot of Carter in the disguise. "An excellent likeness."

Carter smiled. "I'm glad it got to you in time."

"Our friends in Paris are very efficient." A waiter in

a filthy apron lounged up to the table. "A mint tea for my friend, and be quick," Bassam barked, and leaned toward Carter. "Now to the beasts you desire."

The talk was of camels until the waiter returned with the tea and left. When he was well out of earshot, Bassam—a strong, solid man with deep brown eyes set in thick features that matched his bulky frame—drew a slip of paper from his coat.

"I have drawn a map, crude, but it will do. The oases are marked, as you can see, by numbers . . . one, two, and three. This is far better than using names over the radio."

"Radio?" Carter said.

Bassam nodded. "My dragoman is nearby now. He is in touch until we find out what numbers on the backs of these correspond to the numbers of the oases."

Again he dug in his pocket. He arranged four snapshots in front of Carter. The Killmaster moved forward to the edge of his chair, mesmerized by the pictures in front of him.

The men were all bearded, and not too dissimilar. Two of them could have been brothers. Overriding the sudden tension that here, at last, was the target that had eluded him for so long was the sudden fear that, because of the similarity of the men, Ravelle Dressler wouldn't be able to say for sure which was El Adwan.

Carter flipped the photos over. There were numbers marked on the back, 1, 2, 3, and 4.

"There are three oases," he said.

Bassam nodded. "There are only three headed out into the desert. The fourth man left the others at the frontier. We have someone following him, but at last report he didn't appear to be heading anywhere in particular."

"It would help," Carter said, "if these snaps were larger."

"I have thought of that," Bassam said, and slid a large envelope toward Carter. "There are blowups of the photos in there."

A curtain parted to their right at the rear of the café, and a short, bearded, shifty-eyed character moved toward them.

"Achmed," Bassam said, "my dragoman."

The little man slid into the third chair and, at a nod from Bassam, pushed a piece of paper toward Carter. On it were numbers matching the men in the photos to the oases: *1 to 3; 2 to 1; 3 to 2.*

Carter looked up with a frown. "What about number four?"

There was sweat on the dragoman's dark face. His eyes darted from Bassam to Carter and back to his employer again.

"What is it? Speak!" Bassam hissed.

"Bodar lost number four about two miles south of here."

"Here?" Bassam said.

The dragoman nodded. "Bodar came to the hut to inform me—"

Suddenly a look of mild surprise came over the dragoman's face, and his words ceased. He reached back as though to slap at a fly behind him, but his hand never completed the gesture. He fell forward, his face making a dull thud when it hit the table.

The curved hilt of a dagger protruded from between his shoulder blades.

"The curtains!" Bassam hissed, propping the body back up. "I'll take care of this. Go!"

It all happened in an instant.

Before the others in the café were fully aware of what had taken place. Carter was up and through the tacky red curtains of the doorway in back of the chair the Arab had occupied. He found himself in a narrow hallway.

At the far end, a white-robed figure was climbing through an arched window. The Killmaster sprinted down the hall, with the sounds of a near riot beginning in the café behind him.

That could mean only one thing: the dead man had finally been noticed.

Bassam would have to handle it his own way. Carter had to get the assassin before he could get to Abu El Adwan. A second thought also crossed his mind: the man going through the window could be El Adwan himself.

The robed figure dropped from sight beyond the window. Carter vaulted up onto the wide ledge and leaped through. In the air, he gasped and fell much further than he had expected into a walled courtyard.

He stumbled for a moment, caught his balance, and saw the white robe vanishing through an open gateway.

Without thought, Carter tugged the Beretta from beneath his sash and gave chase.

On the opposite side of the gateway was a narrow alley running along the rear of a line of camel stalls. For a moment Carter saw no one. Cautiously, he took a step forward.

Suddenly a figure leaped from the shadows to his right. Carter ducked to the side but was not fast enough. A chopping blow to his right wrist sent the Beretta off into the darkness.

Carter struck blindly with his left. His fist crunched into something soft, and he heard a sharp curse of pain.

Instantly, the Killmaster swung to the right and dropped into a crouch.

At the same time, the killer lurched back so the moonlight fell across his face. The expression on the bearded face was startled with fear and hatred as he swung.

His fist caught the Killmaster in the chest, and then, before he could recoil, the other hand came down open. Sharp fingernails slashed across his cheek. Carter felt warm blood trickle down his chin.

Carter put the full weight of his body behind a killing chop to the neck, which was deflected by a raised shoulder. Suddenly a knee drove up between Carter's legs. He managed to deflect it on his thigh, but it sent him sprawling to the ground. A boot blotted out the moon and came driving down toward Carter's face.

He rolled and managed to grasp toe and ankle. At the same time, Carter came up on one foot and a knee. As the man went forward, the Killmaster brought the ankle down across his knee.

The sound of the ankle cracking merged with the strangled shout of pain. The man kicked out with his other foot and managed to free himself. He rolled over, up against the stone wall, doubled back, and managed somehow to struggle to his feet.

"Stop now or die!" Carter panted in garbled Arabic.

All he got in reply was a growl as the man pushed off the wall toward him.

Carter met him in mid-stride, feinted to the right, and then dropped back. Without missing a beat, he brought his boot up, drop-kick fashion, dead center in the man's gut. He went into the air and Carter caught him full on with the ends of four fingers in the windpipe.

The killer hit the ground, tried to suck in one last gasp of air, and gave it up.

Carter staggered into the shadow of the wall and leaned against it until he could get his breath. Back in the area of the café there were still voices shouting, but, surprisingly, no one seemed to be coming his way.

From the pocket of his pants beneath the robe he dug out a penlight. Falling to his knees beside the body, he tore the four large glossy prints from the envelope.

The dragoman had said that it was number four who had headed toward Dehibat, while the other three had moved in the opposite direction.

He found the picture with the 4 in dark ink on the back of it, and placed it beside the man's face.

No doubt.

Carter had found number four.

He took only enough time to cast the penlight around until he found the Beretta. This done, he stashed everything back under the robes and hurried down the alley. It was a maze, but he could tell from the moon that he was heading in the right direction: toward the open desert.

When he hit it, he made a large circle around the town, keeping high dunes between himself and the flickering lights.

Twenty minutes later he dropped into the wadi. The camp had been all packed up. Ami, one of the Ingrams slung over his shoulder, was by the Land-Rover. Ravelle came up out of the front seat as Carter approached.

"We heart shouting," Ami said, flicking the Ingram's safety back on.

"Trouble," Carter replied, yanking open the passenger side door, "but I don't think it will affect us."

"God, what happened to your face?" Ravelle cried.

"Would you believe a jealous husband?" he growled. "I'll tell you later. Look at this and tell me, please, that it is El Adwan."

He put the photo of number four on her lap and steadied the beam of the penlight. Ravelle took it from his hand and carefully examined the forehead, the area around the eyes, and the neck just below the left earlobe.

"No," she said at last, shaking her head.

"You're sure?"

"Positive."

"Shit."

"What is so important about this one?" she asked.

"Nothing. It would have just made tonight's job one hell of a lot easier if this had been our man."

"Why?"

"Because I just killed him," Carter said, and spread out the other three pictures.

Ravelle sat for several seconds staring at Carter, her face a shade or two lighter than usual.

"Something wrong?" he said. "You look shocked. For God's sake, Ravelle, you knew what we came here to do. Get with it!"

She studied each photograph, one by one, and then started over again. Ami stood stoically by, lovingly carressing the barrel of the Ingram. Carter lit a cigarette and paced. He was just about to give up, to concede that El Adwan had disguised himself well enough to slip away again, when Ravelle called to him.

"Nick . . ."

He lurched to her side. "Yeah?"

"This one."

"Are you absolutely positive?"

She shivered but stuck out her chin. "Look, Nick, isn't this what you brought me along for?"

Carter squeezed her arm. "Sorry."

She held the picture up to the light. "See, here, on his

neck? It's a little lump just under the skin. It's some kind of a growth. You couldn't see it unless it was pointed out to you."

Carter saw it. "Anything else?"

"Here on the left forehead. That little mark."

"A scar . . . tiny, but there," Carter said.

"And here, by his right eye. It's another scar. He said he got it when he was a child."

Carter kissed her. "You're wonderful."

He flipped the picture over. There was a heavy black 3 on the back. He dug out the map and whirled on Ami.

"It's this one . . . he's headed there now!"

The tall Arab nodded and jabbed the map with a finger. "We can drive to here. Ride the rest of the way."

"Let's go!" Carter barked, and crawled into the Land-Rover.

SEVEN

Ami made contact with the Bedouin who had followed number three—Abu El Adwan—soon after they had left the Land-Rover on horseback. In three-minute intervals, he led them in by voice.

Then, in the shadow of high dunes about a mile and a half from the oasis, they spotted him. He somehow blended with the sand, only the blue shine of his rifle and the whiteness of some silver bracelets informing on him.

Ami pressed forward and the two men quickly exchanged information. After a few minutes, he returned to Carter and Ravelle

"He had to follow at a great distance to avoid detection."

"Not with a vehicle, I hope," Carter said.

"No, by camel. The beast is there, about two hundred yards in a wadi. He almost lost your man."

"How so?"

"Adwan joined a small caravan about six miles out."

Carter cursed under his breath. "How big?"

"Five camels and some goats. There are three men and a woman."

"No children?" Carter asked.

"None," Ami replied, tapping the Ingram with his fingers.

"It could be dumb luck on his part, or . . ."

Ami nodded. "It could be an arranged rendezvous."

"What does that mean?" Ravelle asked, her eyes darting between the two men.

"It means," Carter said, "that he's over there in the middle of innocent people, or with a backup guard for himself, or he has already met up with the people that brought him here. Ami, are the others armed?"

"Yes, but only with rifles."

"That doesn't say much. Everyone in the desert carries a rifle. What's the terrain like?"

"There are a series of high, rolling dunes to the south of the oasis. Good cover."

Carter nodded. "All right. We'll circle around to the south to spot them. I take it that the Bedouin's contract ends here?"

Ami nodded.

"Have him take our horses to where his camel is tethered and wait for us there. Ravelle . . ."

"In for a penny, in for a pound," she said. "No reason to sit on the sidelines now."

Minutes later, the Bedouin was leading the horses into

the darkness and Ami was leading them, single file, in a large circle around the oasis.

It seemed forever, but less than thirty minutes later Ami stopped and pointed. "Up there, less than two hundred yards."

Carter passed the heavy Ingram to Ravelle and removed the sand cover from the sniper rifle. In seconds he had locked on the Startron scope and slung the rifle.

"Wait here!"

They both nodded, and Carter started up the side of the dune. With night, a chill had settled over the desert and there was just enough wind to make an eerie, singing sound.

Just short of the top, he dropped to his belly and wiggled on his elbows to the rise.

The oasis was small, a few thorn trees and four clumps of desert palms. There was only one well, and evidently a deep one, evidenced by the total lack of grass or any other surface vegetation that would be spawned by water near the surface.

A makeshift camp had been set up, but the absence of two things bothered Carter. There was no sign of the small, leather tents common to the area. That meant that the group probably didn't plan on camping the entire night. Also, the fire was small, far too small for cooking. A small copper kettle was hung over the flame, and Carter could smell the aroma of tea carried by the wind.

In the light from a sliver of moon, Carter counted. All of them were dressed in dark garduras, a heavy, djellabalike robe with large armholes and a wide girth that could hide almost any kind of weapon.

Three figures crouched by the fire. A fourth busied himself with the animals. Carter noted that girths had been loosened on the camels' bellies, but they had not been unsaddled.

The fifth hunkered at the base of one of the palm clumps, smoking. Now and then the glow of a cigarette gleamed through his cupped hands.

Cautiously, Carter eased the barrel of the Mannlichter over the ridge of sand and fitted his eye to the Startron. Facial features became clear as he moved the scope from figure to figure.

One of the three figures at the fire was the woman. The man smoking at the palms was Abu El Adwan.

Carter eased the arms of the tripod forward and settled the bases into the sand. He locked a cartridge in and thumbed the safety to "off." Slowly he turned the focus ring until a dark spot was clear in the center of Adwan's chest. A quick adjustment of the windage and elevation screws, and he was set.

It took all of Carter's willpower not to take the man out then and there. But it would have been foolhardy and he knew it.

If the other four were El Adwan's backup—and now it was pretty obvious that they were—Carter would be a sitting duck on the dune all by himself. This was especially true since the Mannlichter was only single-action. The moment he fired, the other four would fan out and flank him before he could get off another shot.

He needed Ami and the firepower of the two Ingrams as his own backup.

Reluctantly, he eased the stock of the rifle to the sand and belly-crawled backward down the dune. Halfway, he lurched to his feet and jogged to the bottom.

In hushed tones he explained the situation.

Ami nodded his understanding and spoke with a new

grimness in his voice. "The rendezvous was planned. They are with him."

"I'm afraid so," Carter agreed, "and I'm not surprised. He takes no chances with his own skin."

Hurriedly, Carter gave Ravelle a thirty-second lesson on firing and reloading the Ingram.

"Ami will take my right flank there, and you'll take my left, about seventy-five yards away. All you have to do is spray the area around the campfire. With this thing, you'll hit something. Just remember to keep the barrel down or the gun is liable to dance around and catch Ami or myself. Can you do it?"

She nodded a bit tentatively but gave Carter a little more confidence with the reappearance of the defiant, jutting jaw he now recognized so well.

"Good girl. All right, let's go . . . quietly."

But suddenly there was no such thing as quiet. A humming sound arrested their movement. It quickly became a roar that filled the night. The three of them turned as one.

"There, to the south!" Ami hissed.

"Christ, a chopper!"

Even as Carter stared, the four-seater Bell, its whirling rotors gleaming in the moonlight, rose above the dunes and bore down on them. The machine loomed larger and larger, and suddenly twin landing spots flicked on from just above the sled.

Two hundred yards in front of them, the desert was turned from night into day.

"Quick!" Carter barked. "Spread, flatten out, and cover up completely!"

Ami and Ravelle lurched to the side as Carter dived for the lowest part of the gulley between the two dunes. All three of them went slithering under their robes like insects under rocks.

The Killmaster took quiet, even breaths, not moving a muscle as the sound of the chopper passed directly over him. He took his cue from the dark, the light, and the dark again, as well as the throbbing drone of the chopper's engine as it landed.

"Now!" he cried, bounding to his feet. "Up the dune!"

Carter was the first to the top. Quickly he surveyed the scene, now completely illuminated by the splashing light from beneath the chopper.

The engine was on idle, the rotors turning lazily. The pilot was still at the controls. A passenger—short, balding, in a dark suit and carrying a briefcase—had dropped to the ground. Just as he did, he slipped in the sand and fell to one knee, the light bathing his face and shoulders.

Carter heard a gasp from Ravelle and a few feet to his left, but he kept his eyes on the tableau.

The small man moved toward El Adwan, who stood in the center of the other robed figures. There was little doubt now as to who the woman and three other men of the caravan actually were.

Each of them had produced Russian AK-47 rifles from beneath their desert robes.

Carter moved the Mannlichter around to focus on El Adwan. He adjusted the scope and squinted. Even though the man was stationary, he was constantly shielded by the restless guards.

The chopper's passenger reached him and they shook hands. They exchanged a few words and nods.

Carter sweated and waited.

Then they moved farther away from the chopper and into the darkness until there was just the two of them. But El Adwan walked on the far side, with the small, balding man between himself and Carter with the sniper rifle.

The Killmaster readjusted the focus and range. It was about two hundred and fifty yards, with very little wind.

An easy shot.

A sure kill shot.

If the two men would only change places.

The minutes dragged on. The pilot in the chopper looked bored. Two of the guards dropped into a crouch and lit cigarettes. The woman wandered over to the chopper and exchanged a few words with the pilot.

Carter sweated some more, the tension building to a knot in his chest. With one finger he cleared the perspiration from his forehead and quickly returned it to the trigger. On either side of him he swore that he could hear Ami and Ravelle breathing.

Suddenly the balding man dropped to one knee. He set the briefcase on the ground and opened it. A tiny blub came on, evidently powered by a battery within the case.

Furiously, Carter sighted in: focus right, elevation right, windage set, range. . . .

But before he could fire, El Adwan also went down, to his butt, so his entire body was once again obscured by the other man.

Carter cursed under his breath and tried to focus on the terrorist's bobbing head.

It was no good.

He chanced a quick glance at his watch, shielding the luminous dial with his hand.

The helicopter had been on the ground for twenty minutes.

He swiveled his eyes to Ravelle. She was game, the Ingram cradled in front of her, ready. She appeared calm.

To Carter's right, Ami appeared to be dozing, but the Killmaster could tell the truth of it when now and then he saw the muzzle swerve around to cover one of the moving guards.

El Adwan was up, shoving a package into his clothing. But so was the other man.

They started moving back toward the chopper, the terrorist still blocked by his companion.

Carter moved the muzzle of the rifle ahead of them. He was guessing. At the chopper, they would shake hands again. Then the balding man would climb in. For just that second, when the man was getting seated, El Adwan would be completely exposed.

For the last time, Carter adjusted the scope.

They reached the door. Just as Carter guessed, they shook hands. A few more words were exchanged, and the small man set his briefcase on the floorboards in front of the seat. He grasped the hand pull, put his right foot on the step, and pulled himself up.

Carter took a deep breath, eased it out, and fired.

"Damn!" Carter growled aloud.

The man's foot had slipped on the step, throwing him backward. In that instant, El Adwan had stepped forward to balance him.

It was just far enough.

The balding man had taken the heavy-caliber slug from the Mannlichter, and the loud crack of the rifle had resounded over the gentle idle of the chopper's engine. They were all alerted and they swung immediately into action.

Two of the four guards dropped to one knee and sprayed the ridge in Carter's direction with their rifles. The other two, one of them the woman, raced to the flanks, firing on the run.

The Ingram in Ami's hand was bucking, firing at the

running figure on his side. But missing.

There was silence from Carter's left. The woman was frozen.

"Fire, Ravelle, dammit! Fire at anything!" Carter shouted, jamming another cartridge into the sniper rifle.

El Adwan had been galvanized into action himself, but not defensive. As usual, his first thought was himself.

He had wrenched the dead man around in front of him. Then, using the other man's body as a shield, he was now crawling into the chopper. Carter could see him barking orders at the pilot, and he knew exactly what those orders were.

The engine was roaring now and the rotors were picking up speed.

Carter sighted in on the pilot's head. It was a tough shot, almost impossible. The slugs from the two kneeling guards were kicking up sand all around Carter's head and the chopper was moving, lifting off the desert floor.

Wisely, the pilot was jiggling the machine from side to side as he got lift. El Adwan had brought his own rifle into play and was firing at the orange spurts that Ami's Ingram made in the night.

Then Carter got some peace and quiet. Ami had zeroed in on the two squatting guards. With a fanning burst he had raked them, sending them both flying backward to land, very dead, spread-eagled in the sand.

It was the lull the Killmaster needed. He sighted in. The chopper was about twenty-five feet off the ground and rolling its tail around. When the spin was completed, the silhouette of the pilot was dead center in Carter's sights.

He fired, and through the scope saw the pilot's head explode, the remnants spraying the far side of the Plexiglás bubble.

It was a perfect hit, but the Killmaster had other problems. The female guard, realizing that she was drawing no fire, had made a right angle and charged up the dune. Carter's shot drew her and she turned his way.

Suddenly she was charging over the rim, the bucking AK-47 in her hand on full auto.

Carter managed to roll away from the first burst as he struggled to get another cartridge into the Mannlichter.

Even as he jammed the bolt home, he knew he would be too late. The woman had spotted him and read the situation. She skidded to a halt and brought the muzzle of the gun around in a slowly deliberate motion.

At the last second, just before she fired, her eyes went wide and the rifle dropped from her hands. Carter heard the chatter of Ravelle's Ingram just as the woman's body lifted into the air and fell, lifeless, at his side.

He looked up. Ravelle knelt only two feet behind where the woman had been, her face stark white, the Ingram still shaking in her hands.

"I'm sorry," she gasped.

"Better late than never," Carter said, leaping toward her.

He grabbed the Ingram and a magazine from the belt around her chest. In one movement he had reloaded and turned.

The chopper was still rising, slowly spinning in circles. He raised the Ingram and fired.

Halfway through the clip, he saw the hatch open. A body came through it and hurtled down to hit the sand. In the same instant, the chopper righted. The nose bent, the tail lifted, and it moved off.

Carter finished the magazine, but it was too late. In seconds the machine was over a dune and lifting into the night sky.

"You son of a bitch!" Carter screamed, watching it disappear.

El Adwan had kicked out the pilot's body and taken the controls himself.

Carter had lost again.

But even in his anger, his instincts took over. As the sound of the chopper faded, he realized that all around him was deathly silence.

Mentally he made a body count: two dead in the sand near where the chopper had been, and the woman's mangled corpse at his feet.

"Ami?"

A long silence and then, "Down here," from the gulley behind the far end of the dune.

Carter grabbed another clip from Ravelle and jacked it in as he ran.

Ami stood, a bloody dagger in his hand, carefully shredding the sleeve over his right arm. The top of the sleeve was crimson.

At his feet was the fourth guard, his head nearly severed from his body.

"You're hit," Carter said.

Ami nodded, making bandages from the ripped cloth.

"Bad?"

The man shook his head.

"Let the woman give you a hand with the bandage. I'll do the burying."

Still without a word, the big Arab moved off.

Carter found tools in the packs of the camels and went to work. It took the better part of two hours to erase all traces of the battle. During that time, the little man who had been their spotter wandered in, leading the three horses and his camel.

When the burying was done, Carter went through the packs and saddlebags of all the camels, and re-checked the area.

Nothing.

El Adwan had once again gotten away clean.

They were just mounting for the ride back to the Land-Rover, when Ravelle grasped Carter's arm.

"I did the best I could," she said, still looking a little sick.

Carter squeezed her shoulder. "You came through just when you had to. That's more than enough. This isn't exactly your line of work."

"There is one thing that may help . . ."

"What's that?"

"The bald man, the one who came in the helicopter?"

"Yes?" Carter said, his antennae coming out as he remembered the gasp he had heard when the man with the briefcase had dropped into the light. "What about him?"

"I recognized him. It was Oliver Estes."

EIGHT

St. James Manor sat regally on two hundred acres of lush Surrey contryside south of London. Heavy-coated sheep and fat cattle ranged on the deep green fields, and the whole was surrounded by chest-high stone fences. Nearer the manor proper, the fences were three feet higher, with electrified wire and glass shards around the top.

The house itself was a massive two-story Tudor in the shape of an L. Heavy dark beams contrasted sharply with the whitewashed walls, and the windows, set deeply, were of heavy leaded glass.

From the road, a wide gravel carriage lane wound through manicured lawns and gardens with tall, graceful trees, past a pond in which ducks and geese and swans swam freely during the summer months.

Hannibal St. James sat behind his massive desk in his massive swivel chair in his massive second-story office.

The great man was a vision in gray—dapper gray tweeds, pearl-gray shirt, dark gray tie, pale gray eyes, and silver-gray hair.

Only one thing marred the image of the world-shaking tycoon in his own element: Hannibal St. James was sweating like the proverbial pig. Now and then, between large sips of cognac from the snifter in his right hand, he would mop the dew from his face with a monogrammed handkerchief in his left.

St. James had a lot to sweat about. It had been thirty-six hours since the meeting in the desert, and he had received no word. Everything depended on that filthy Arab's agreement to his end of the bargain. St. James had agreed on the price: ten million . . . five in front, five on completion.

Where was Oliver Estes?

Behind the wall to his right, the telex machines began to clatter. The sound made St. James jump in his chair.

It had been a telex earlier that afternoon, using his private code, that had started his sweat glands going:

TONIGHT EIGHT P.M. SHARP YOUR TIME.
PRIVATE HOT LINE TO YOUR OFFICE
WILL CALL. BE THERE. ESTES.

St. James glanced at the diamond-encrusted watch on his wrist: 7:55.

The telex didn't sound like Estes at all. Oliver would never have the nerve to make such an imperative command: *Be there*.

But perhaps Estes was up to his old tricks. Perhaps

the man actually thought he had found a foolproof way to betray St. James.

Impossible, he thought, gulping the last of the cognac. *I would make sure he died a horrible death if it was the last thing I did!*

He took a cigarette from an oblong crystal box on the desk. He inserted it into an ivory holder and lit it with a gold lighter. His movements were uncharacteristically shaky and the smoke burned his lungs.

The door opened silently and closed the same way. Horst Layman moved across the room and eased his huge bulk into a leather chair.

"Anything more on the wire?"

"Nothing," Layman grunted. The big man's eyes were like a cat's: the concentrated pupils tiny, the irises large, the gaze absolutely unfathomable.

The telephone buzzed and St. James forced himself to wait several seconds before answering it.

"Yes?"

"Hannibal St. James?"

"Yes. Who is this? How did you get my private telex code and this number?"

"From Oliver Estes," the voice said, "before he died."

"Estes is dead?"

"As dead as anyone can be after taking a high-powered slug in his back."

"Damn . . ."

The voice calmly gave St. James a complete rundown on the happenings in the Tunisian desert thirty-six hours before.

"But in spite of the problems and your man's death, Mr. St. James, I have decided to go ahead with the contract. There will be, however, some new stipulations."

St. James froze. "I have met every one of your demands. It is not my fault that you have an American agent on your back from your earlier affairs!"

"Mr. St. James, you know who and what I am."

"I do."

"And now I know who and what you are. Besides buying my silence, what I am about to ask of you will provide me with a much better atmosphere to carry out your contract."

"I don't want myself, or anyone connected with me, to be involved!"

"You will not be involved in the contract."

St. James's voice shook when he replied. "What the hell do you call killing an American agent? If that is not 'involvement,' then I don't know what is! Besides, if the man is as good as you say he is, how in God's name could my people get close to him?"

"I have a plan all worked out. For the last two days I have done nothing but gather information. I know that the woman with Carter was Ravelle Dressler. Now, here is what I want your people to do . . ."

As Abu El Adwan spoke, Hannibal St. James removed the cigarette from the ivory holder and tapped it out, gently, in an alabaster ashtray. The disembodied voice through the phone was like the voice of a ghost at a seance. But he found himself listening raptly.

"It might work," St. James said when the voice ceased.

"Of course it will work. And it will also buy me the needed time. I assume the *Thor I* is still on the timetable given me by Mr. Estes?"

"It is. The ship sails the day after tomorrow from Japan for the Middle East."

"Keep Carter off my back, Mr. St. James. Buy me the

time, and your contract will be completed."

Hannibal St. James glanced up at Horst Layman's flat, vacuous face, and nodded. "We will do it, exactly as you say."

"Good. If Carter thinks I'm in London, he won't be looking for me anywhere else. I'll make the phone call to Ravelle Dressler the day after tomorrow at this same hour. That should give your people enough time to prepare."

The line went dead, and St. James sat back in his chair with a sigh. He tapped the tips of his fingers together in front of his face and stared at Horst Layman, who stared back impassively.

When St. James spoke, it was in a quiet, almost dull monotone. He went on for a full fifteen minutes, and when he finished, Horst Layman only nodded.

He stood and lumbered toward the door. It would be a very busy two days.

The huge man gave no thought to the victim. The name Nick Carter meant nothing to him, no more than the fact that the man was an American government agent.

Nick Carter was a man. He would die as all men die.

In an outdoor phone booth in Rome's Piazza del Popolo, a tall, dark-skinned priest with a bald spot on the back of his head hung up the phone. After looking around, he moved out of the box and walked at a leisurely pace down the street. He walked across the Ponte Margherita, and followed the Tiber around the Castel Sant'Angelo. Several blocks farther on, he turned into the Via della Conciliazione. Two blocks short of Saint Peter's Square, he stopped at a newly renovated building.

A key opened the front door and he stepped into a

marbled lobby. Shunning the elevator, he walked up four flights and let himself into an apartment with a second key.

The apartment was huge, expensive, and tasteful. The living room was filled with ebony and copper bookcases covering three entire walls. On the far wall, separating the windows and the fireplace, were priceless copies of two sixteenth-century Italian enamel portraits. The room was dark, the windows heavily draped with deep blue brocade.

Unbuttoning his dark suit jacket and sliding it from his shoulders, he moved on into the bedroom. Like the living room, it was exquisite, characterized by rich patterns, colors, and textures. Natural wood boiserie with Cordoba leather panels warmed the room and set off the black marble mantel that dominated one entire wall.

The huge canopied bed where he discarded the rest of the priest's garb was draped in royal blue velvet trimmed with embroidery. A huge antique Chinese carpet in shades of blue and rose covered most of the highly polished parquet floor.

Abu El Adwan enjoyed luxury no matter what the cost.

From a mini-bar he poured himself a cognac and entered the bathroom. After a long shower, he donned red socks, tan slacks, low boots with Cuban heels, and a bright knit shirt. From a drawer, he got a cheap camera and a pair of lightly tinted glasses.

These would help him assume the guise of a tourist-about-town later that evening.

A catch in one wall opened two panels. El Adwan stepped back to make the evening's choice.

Long ago, he had spent time with a master wigmaker and makeup specialist who had retired from the Kabuki

theater. During that time, El Adwan had studied well and
purchased even better.

Now before him on a huge wall board were over two
hundred wigs of every imaginable length, texture, and
color. There were also matching mustaches, beards,
sideburns, and even eyebrows and eyelashes.

He selected a sandy-brown wig with matching eyebrows, sideburns, and a heavy mustache. When the facial
hair was meticulously applied with a spirit gum, he discarded the black wig of the balding priest and donned
the new one.

Finished, he stared at himself in the mirror and smiled.
Nobody in the world could recognize him; he hardly
recognized himslef. And the spirit gum was made especially for him from an old Greek formula. It adhered
directly to the pores in the skin. He could do anything
in the disguise—swim, shower, yank and pull—and nothing would happen. When he was through with the disguise, he had to use a special solvent to remove it.

A few final touches were needed. He used a stain to
slightly discolor his white teeth. Two thin rubber pads
between cheek and gum subtly altered the shape of his
face.

He slipped into a plaid sports jacket and adjusted the
collar of the shirt over the jacket. From a case containing
over forty pairs of tinted contact lenses, he chose a pair
that he laughingly called "Paul Newman" blue, and inserted them.

With a last look in the mirror, he draped the camera
around his neck and left the apartment.

The man with the strikingly blue eyes and the loud
clothes moved swiftly down the deserted hotel corridor.

The odor of decay hung like a stagnant cloud near the low ceiling of the narrow passageway. The only sound reaching his ears came from the creak of the slowly rotting boards beneath his feet.

There were no windows in the hallway, and the single bulb burning at the end of a frayed cord strained to push every one of its fifteen watts through the thick atmosphere. For all the light available, he could have been in Rome's catacombs instead of a run-down hotel on the Appia Antica.

It was called Il Grande Appia, but on the street it was nicknamed La Puttana—the Prostitute—because most of its tenents were ladies of the street. It was a home for losers, a last stop for society's rejects, a graveyard for the living. The place was too dreary to stay in if one didn't have to, which was why he had chosen it for the meeting.

He slowed his pace as he neared the last room at the end of the hallway, but quickly jumped aside when a squeaking rat darted from one hole in the woodwork to another. He watched the rat pass, chuckled, and then turned to the door.

It was marked MAINTENANCE—NO ADMITTANCE.

The door was unlocked. Beyond it was a steep set of unlit stairs. In the glow of a cigarette lighter, he descended and rapped on a second door at the bottom.

''*Sí?*''

"Jadak?"

"Who wants to know?"

"Abu, my friend . . . the wealthy tourist who has come to make you rich."

Bolts were pulled aside and the door opened a few inches. Behind it was a tall lanky figure in a shabby topcoat. His thick black hair was worn long and brushed back from his forehead.

"Jesus Christ, how do I know it is you? I never see you the same twice!"

Abu El Adwan smiled. The man who stood before him was Jadak Salas, and he had worked closely with El Adwan twice in the past. But, like everyone else, he had no idea what Adwan really looked like.

Slowly, in almost a whisper, El Adwan recited the names of the other ten men and two women in the basement room behind Jadak.

"Mother of Christ, come in." He stepped into the room and the door was closed and locked behind him. Jadak turned to the hard-eyed, expectant faces. "Believe it or not, this is Abu El Adwan."

One of the women, a young blonde with eyes like cold steel, couldn't stifle a giggle.

"You, my dear Antonia Perini, should recognize my voice, at least. How many nights did I whisper words of love while I thrust between your thighs, two years ago on Malta?"

"Sweet Jesus," the blonde gasped, and crossed herself.

The others laughed, and El Adwan made his way to the front of the room. Even as he moved, the inner man emerged through the disguise and the room fell silent.

"You have all agreed to the terms, so from this night on you are in, and there is no getting out. Do I make myself understood?"

A chorus of affirmative grunts.

"Each of you is a specialist at more than one thing. All of your talents will be well used, I assure you."

"Who are we killing for this time?" asked a male voice from the rear.

El Adwan smiled. "As always, oppressed peoples everywhere."

"Bullshit," said the second woman, a short, very voluptuous brunette, and laughed harshly.

"What do we call ourselves?" asked another.

Another wide smile from El Adwan. "I'm sure that between us we can find an appropriate political name for our cause."

"Quiet," Jadak hissed. "I for one want to know the game!"

The room became gravely silent and all eyes turned to the front.

"The fourteen of us are going to hijack the largest ship in the world, the brand-new supertanker, *Thor I*."

NINE

Her eyes were a smoldering gray and deep-set, so that they enhanced her cheekbones into a strong angle that gave off an accurate impression of self-willed self-sufficiency and self-reliance.

But at this moment Carolyn Reed felt far from self-reliant. She felt confused and scared.

It had been five days since she had taken the phone call from Ishu Tanaki in the hotel room in Japan. She had sat for hours, her bags packed, waiting for him, until the room had closed in and she had to do something.

At four in the morning, she had taken a cab to his tiny, transient apartment. The old *mama-san* had ranted, but finally the woman had let Carolyn in. They had found the money and the note, but nothing else.

Carolyn had returned to the hotel and waited until noon. Still Tanaki hadn't shown.

That was when she had called Sir Charles Dunwood, her superior in London. Sir Charles was the head of the very quiet arm of Lloyd's known as Insuree Investigations. He had been as troubled as she about Ishu Tanaki.

"Should I inform the police?"

"My dear Carolyn, what could you tell them?"

Carolyn had bridled. How like Sir Charles and his damnable cautiousness. In her mind, Ishu had found something big, and just at the moment he had been ready to pass it on to her and leave the Thor Project for the last time, he had disappeared. As far as she was concerned, it was no time for caution: it was time for action.

But Sir Charles Dunwood made the decisions.

"I suggest that you return to London at once, Carolyn. I think for the time being, a waiting game is preferable. I have a great many friends in the Home Office. I suggest we make some discreet inquiries in that area."

So Carolyn had returned. She had filed her report and reiterated Ishu Tanaki's last words over the phone.

So far, nothing had happened. But that afternoon Sir Charles had dropped by her office.

"I know this is highly irregular, my dear, but I wonder if I might drop by your flat this evening?"

"Of course, but—"

"A private discussion."

"Of course."

"Shall we say, ten?"

Carolyn shifted her eyes from the mirror to the clock on a nearby mantel.

It was one minute before ten.

Absently, she watched the second hand sweep around. When it reached the top, a single chime announced the hour. The sound had scarcely faded when the doorbell buzzed.

How like Sir Charles, punctual to the second, she thought as she walked to the door on long, supple legs.

"Sir Charles, good evening."

Sir Charles Dunwood bowed slightly and stepped into the foyer. He was a mustached man in his late fifties, with graying hair closely cropped, a military bearing, and the stern face of command. He wore a tweed suit with matching vest, a regimental tie perfectly knotted at his throat, and gave the impression that he would much rather be in uniform.

Dunwood had started his career in the Scots Guards, and gravitated to the Home Office as liaison to MI5 and MI6. Upon his early retirement, he had taken over the investigative section of Lloyd's.

"Beastly weather," he said, handing Carolyn his hat, raincoat, and umbrella.

"Yes, yes, it is. A drink?"

"A gin, if you have it."

Of course I have it, Carolyn thought gratingly as she walked to the sideboard. *What civilized English household could survive without gin?*

She prepared the drinks and they sat. For a full five minutes the conversation was inane, and Carolyn thought she would scream.

At last Sir Charles leaned forward and got to the point. "The Japanese authorities were informed of Tanaki's disappearance through my friends in the Home Office, and, in turn, a branch of MI6."

"And . . . ?"

"Nothing. It is as if he had never existed. They have suggested that he may have fled on his own. As you know, he was not happy in his role as a junior investigator under you."

Carolyn folded her hands in her lap with great control. Taking a deep breath, she lifted her head and looked Sir Charles in the eye. Something had blazed and hardened, like the effect of an intense fire.

"I cannot accept that, Sir Charles. I will not accept it. Ishu and I worked out those differences between us, particularly when we began getting results on the *Thor* investigation."

"You've never actually stated a theory, Carolyn. What do you think?"

She couldn't stop a shiver from running through her body. To cover it, she grabbed the glasses and made fresh drinks. By the time she had seated herself again, control had returned.

"I think Ishu had obtained facts. I think he had uncovered a plot to doom the *Thor* before she ever sailed. And if she did sail, I think there is a plot to sink her."

Sir Charles sipped his drink and rubbed the loose skin on his temple. "I assumed that was your conclusion. And Tanaki?"

"I think . . . I think he was killed to stop him from passing his findings along to me."

"My dear, what you're saying borders on the impossible. If it is true, and it corresponds to your earlier reports, such a plan would have to originate at the very top . . . perhaps with Hannibal St. James himself!"

Carolyn swallowed and straightened her shoulders. "That's exactly what I think."

Suddenly Sir Charles smiled. "If it is any help, Carolyn,

I am in total agreement with you."

She was instantly on her feet. "Then why—"

"I addressed the board with both findings and theories this afternoon."

"And . . . ?"

"And they have decided that the findings are inconclusive and the theories implausible. We must remember that St. James Lines have over ninety vessels insured with us."

"So what? All ninety would be a drop in the bucket if the *Thor* goes down and we pay the insured!"

"True."

"Then they are going to stand by—"

"They, my dear, are. *We* are not."

Carolyn slumped heavily back into her chair. "But what can we do?"

"Perhaps a great deal. This is Friday. I am meeting two very powerful gentlemen at my club on Monday for lunch. I think I have enough information to interest them in our problem."

"How can you be so sure?"

"Because they have already expressed undue interest as of noon today in one of the chief architects of the Thor Project, Oliver Estes."

"St. James's comptroller?"

"Yes," Sir Charles said. "The inquiries were subtle but demanding. My guess is that the Thor Project has come under suspicion by several people beyond our sphere."

A new light came into Carolyn Reed's eyes. "Then you think that by giving them all the information we've found . . ."

Again Sir Charles nodded, this time far more emphat-

ically. "Her Majesty's Government has far more weight
with the International Maritime Commission than we do."

"And in the meantime?"

"In the meantime, the *Thor* has been inspected again,
and again cleared. She sails tomorrow morning."

"Oh, my God."

A few minutes later, Sir Charles excused himself and
left.

Carolyn Reed went to bed, but she didn't sleep. Each
time she closed her eyes she could see the enormous bow
of the *Thor* slipping beneath the water as millions of
barrels of oil from her ruptured tanks polluted the sea for
miles around.

Ravelle Dressler ran her fingertips over the pale blue
circles beneath her eyes and growled at the mirror as she
had practically every night since their return.

She felt more like a prisoner now in the Mayfair flat
than she had before.

"We'll give you a guard or an escort whenever you
want to go out," Carter had said.

"No, I don't want a baby-sitter . . . unless it's you."

"Ravelle, I'm still after him. I've still got to get him."

"Okay, all right. I'll be fine."

But she wasn't fine. She was drinking too much, and
even though she knew she was safe, she found herself
jumping at every shadow and every sound. And sleep
was hard. When it did come, she relived the desert in a
nightmare, only to wake up in a cold sweat.

Maybe she should go to America . . . New York, or
even Montana. God knows the Arab bastard wouldn't
follow her there.

Or would he?

She kicked open the dressing room door. The room was stacked with suitcases and garment bags bloated with clothing. She had packed and repacked a dozen times, and still couldn't bring herself to go.

Ravelle dug two aspirin tablets out of her medicine chest and washed them down with gin. She stepped into the chilling shower and, after emitting a slight scream, began to bathe.

Three minutes was all she could take. When her body was dry and powdered, she used the blow dryer on her hair until she could no longer stand the noise. Then she slipped into a robe and walked across the flat to the kitchen.

"You've got to eat while you drink," she told herself, and dropped two eggs into a pan before returning to the living room and more gin.

The glass was half full when the telephone rang. Absently, she lifted it with her left hand.

"Yes?"

"Ravelle, you are such a bitch . . ."

"Oh, my God, you!" The bottle of gin fell, its contents spreading a stain across the rug.

"Yes, me, Ravelle. I am in London and I'm going to get you. I'm going to kill you, very, very slowly. It might take me some time, but eventually I'll get to you, Ravelle. Until then, wait . . . wait and sweat."

The phone went dead and Ravelle stood for several seconds, shaking, staring at the instrument in her hand.

Then she slammed it back onto its cradle and ran to her purse. Frantically, she clawed at the contents until she found the number Carter had given her.

"What we can ascertain about El Adwan—and about

the people we know he has used in the past—is sketchy. However, one thread runs through the whole: none of them originally came from poverty. As self-appointed terrorists and executioners, none of them was forced into his role by poverty or need. In fact they all came from wealthy families. As nearly as I can tell, their fanaticism has no roots in any specific cause.''

"Then, what can you come up with, Doctor?" Carter asked, blinking the sand of weariness from his eyes.

"I'd say they were all political poseurs, whose enemy was life. In short, they are murderers by personal choice, psychopaths who camouflage their motives behind a smoke screen of utopian theory.''

''Common criminals,'' Carter growled.

"Exactly. The power is the key . . . the power to inflict pain and to terrify.''

"And that includes Abu El Adwan?"

"Most definitely. He has what I would call 'the Hitler complex,' yet he knows he can never rule as Hitler did, so he settles for fame—or infamy, in this case.''

"But for these bigger and grander acts of terrorism," Carter offered, "he must have more and more funds to maintain himself and his deeds."

The psychiatrist nodded.

Carter continued. "All right. Up to now, we have concentrated on El Adwan himself. What if we concentrate on his sources, his contacts, strangle his source of power?"

The doctor shrugged. "What did Hitler do in the bunker?"

Jonathan Hart-Davis groaned. "Would that we were so lucky. Thank you very much, Dr. Boscom."

The eminent psychiatrist and lecturer stood. "Gentlemen, if I can be of any further service . . ."

Carter watched the tall, graying scholar walk from the room, and shook his head. "I don't think we know any more than we knew before."

"Maybe we do," David Hawk said, chomping on the wet butt of a cigar and shuffling a ream of papers in front of him. "We can assume that Oliver Estes had something to do with putting Ravelle Dressler and El Adwan—under the alias of Rahib Salubar—together."

Hart-Davis chimed in. "And within a week after El Adwan completed his dual murders in London, St. James Lines were granted huge petroleum shipping contracts from various small Persian Gulf governments."

"That would suggest collusion, a trade-off," Hawk continued. "Hard to prove, but there nevertheless."

Carter rubbed his red-rimmed eyes and gulped more coffee. They had been at it for three days in the MI-6 war room, and as far as he could see, they were just going around in circles.

"Okay," he said at last, "if Ravelle was correct and it was Oliver Estes that I killed, that means that Estes and El Adwan were cooking up a deal."

"And that means," Hawk said, "that Hannibal St. James is really cooking up the deal. Estes doesn't go to the toilet without getting permission from St. James first. What about Estes's own dossier?"

Owen Hamilton of MI5 had been sitting back, puffing his pipe and listening. Now he leaned forward with a heavy frown on his face. "We've checked him thoroughly . . . office, friends, servants, his club, even the pub he occasionally frequents. He has no family."

"And . . . ?"

"Gone, hasn't been seen. The story is the same from everyone, even his doctor. Stress, too much work. He's on an extended holiday for rest and can't be reached."

"As far as I'm concerned," Hawk growled, "that does it. We know El Adwan is planning something big. He's put the word out for people. And I think it's a sure thing that whatever he's got planned is being financed by Hannibal St. James."

"So all we have to do," Hart-Davis said, "is find out what it is, stop it, and prove St. James had a hand in it!"

The eyes of everyone in the room turned to Nick Carter. The Killmaster was about to reply, when an aide stepped quietly into the room.

"Mr. Carter, I know you're not to be disturbed, but—"

"Yes, what is it?"

"The Dressler woman, sir, she's on the phone. She's demanding to speak to you and she won't take no for an answer. She's a bit hysterical, sir. She says that El Adwan is in London."

Carter was out of his chair in an instant. "Excuse me, gentlemen."

He followed the aide down a brightly lit hallway and into the small cubicle he had been using as an office for the past three days.

"Line three, sir."

"Is it on record?"

"Oh, yes, sir. Every incoming call is recorded."

Carter nodded and grabbed the phone. "Ravelle . . . ?"

"Nick, he called not more than five minutes ago . . ." Her voice was breathless, not hysterical but on the verge.

"Ravelle, please . . ."

"He's in London! He said he's going to get me, kill me! He said even if it takes time . . . no matter how much time, he'll wait, and when the time comes, he'll kill me!"

"Ravelle," Carter barked, "dammit, calm down!" He

paused, listened to the raspy breathing subside on the other end of the line, and continued. "That's better. Now, tell me exactly what he said."

She did, slowly and deliberately, and the Killmaster, even though all of it was going on tape, made notes to himself.

"All right, hold on for a second." He put his hand over the mouthpiece and spoke to the young MI6 officer. "Get me a car ready right away."

"Yes, sir."

"Ravelle, are you in your flat?"

"Yes."

"And the doors are locked?"

"Yes."

"All right, you're safe. It's broad daylight outside and the sun is shining."

"Nick . . ."

"Listen. I'll be there in twenty minutes to a half hour. Does that make you feel better?"

"Yes."

"You're sure it was El Adwan?"

"Positive."

"Hang in there—I'm on my way."

Carter hung up and headed for the elevators. A big four-door Rover was awaiting him in the basement garage. He quickly signed for it and pulled out onto Whitehall. The traffic was heavy up to Trafalgar Square where he cut left to Pall Mall. Just as he turned right on Marlborough Road, a taxi darted out of a narrow lane on his left.

Carter tried to evade, but a bus coming head-on in the other lane made it impossible to avoid a fender-bender.

Instantly, a dark little man—Indian or Pakistani, Carter

guessed—was out of the taxi and shaking his fist at the Killmaster. He was railing in garbled English and a language Carter couldn't immediately decipher.

"It was your own bloody fault," Carter hissed, climbing out of the Rover and moving to the front to check the damage.

"Ah, American, that's it. You were on the wrong side of the road! Americans no drive in England."

Carter ignored him. The left front fender of the Rover was curled into the tire. If he went on, the tire would be flat within a block.

In the meantime, a gawking crowd had gathered and the man—Carter had identified the alternate language now as Urdu—was rising to new heights of hyperbole.

For the next ten minutes Carter tried to calm him down, to no avail. Finally a bobby arrived and Carter was able to show his credentials. Even then it was another twenty minutes before he was able to get a cab and continue on his way.

TEN

Ravelle hung up the phone and leaned against the wall. The room was beginning to spin.

Got to get dressed, she thought, *got to get out of here . . . get dressed, when Nick comes I'll have him take me . . . someplace.*

She staggered into the bedroom, discarding the robe as she moved. Somehow, with trembling fingers, she managed the underwear and then a pair of slacks. A sweater was halfway over her head when she heard the noise. Quickly, she pulled the sweater all the way down.

There were two of them just emerging from the closet. The first one was huge, the most enormous man she had ever seen. The second one was small, wiry, with dark skin and a heavy mustache.

But it was the big one who scared her. His eyes were crazy and drool spilled from his lips as he leered at her.

And then it struck her. They were coming from the closet, from the passageway to the apartment below that Rahib Salubar had used to kill the man.

But how? It had been boarded up, closed off. . . .

Suddenly desperate, Ravelle lunged for the door. The big man flung himself at her in a football tackle. He caught her just over the knees and they went down struggling.

His breath was foul with alcohol and for a few seconds he seemed unsteady. Ravelle was a big, strong woman, and for a time the match seemed comparatively even. Then she managed to sink her teeth deeply into his hand and she was free.

She rolled away from him and ran into the living room. But the little man cut off her path to the front door. She whirled to the bar and snatched a bottle of gin by the neck.

With the big man coming toward her, she crashed the bottom of the bottle against the edge of the bar. Now she had a lethal weapon.

Slowly they circled one another, with not a word passing between them. Each time he tried to get closer, Ravelle lashed out with the jagged edge of the bottle. Finally she reached too far and he came up under her arm.

The bottle flew from her hand to crash against the wall, and a sledgehammer fist buried itself in her belly.

She fell to the floor gasping for air, with the big man on top of her. He was ripping at her sweater, but the little man was pulling him away.

"No, dammit, Horst, not now! Let's get her below. I unlocked the front door."

She had regained her breathing. They forced her,

struggling, across the room. One of them gripped her with both hands. The other held her ankles. Ravelle opened her mouth to let out a long, low scream, but the giant backhanded her before she could make a sound. She felt a spurt of blood from her lips.

Then she was being lowered roughly into darkness. She slipped from their grasp. Her head hit something hard and the darkness was inside her head.

Carter emerged from the elevator at a brisk walk. Even at that distance he could see that Ravelle's door was ajar. He pulled Wilhelmina from the rig under his left armpit and hit the door full bore.

One quick look told him that he was too late. A minute later he had checked all the rooms and grabbed the phone. In no time he was asking for Claude Dakin in the MI6 war room. This would be a job for Special Branch.

"Claude, Nick . . . they've got her."

"Who . . . El Adwan?"

"Looks like it. Get a team over here right away. I'm checking below. They can't have gotten far."

"Will do."

"And, Claude, get in touch with traffic control in the Pall Mall area. I had an accident with a staff car. Hit a taxi, number A47-91184. Have them hold the driver."

Carter hit the hallway and raced toward the service elevator. A woman in a maid's uniform came out of the service stair doors just as he passed.

"Excuse me, is this your floor?"

"This and the one above, sir. Some of the tenants have their own private maids."

"What floor were you working this afternoon?"

"This afternoon? Here, sir."

"Did you see anything or hear anything unusual? A scream, perhaps?"

"No, sir, nothing."

The elevator came and Carter dived into it. On the ground floor, he checked the rear doors and the alley, then the basement garage. When he found nothing, he moved back inside and hit the doorman.

"Did you see Mrs. Dressler leave this afternoon?"

"No, sir. Fact is, haven't seen the lady for three days. Has her groceries sent in, she does."

"Any deliveries today?"

"None, sir."

"What about deliveries to the other flats?"

"A few, some are still there." He motioned to a table laden with packages. "We don't let delivery men go up to the flats, sir. We take delivery ourselves and then take them up to the tenants."

So much for that, Carter thought, and nervously lit a cigarette. "How about workmen? Are there any workmen in the building today?"

"Yes, sir. Pair of chaps working on the air-conditioning units in the basement."

"Which way?"

The man pointed and Carter ran.

It was futile. The two workmen were filthy from cleaning vents, and legit.

By the time Carter got back to the lobby, one Special Branch team had already gone up. He met Claude Dakin with a second team at the elevators.

"I checked the help. No one has seen them take her out. But the service area at the rear is wide open."

Dakin tapped two of the team. "Check the streets outside . . . news vendors, taxi stands, everything."

They nodded and left.

"Your cabdriver was a phony," Dakin said as the elevator rose. "He needed to call his office shortly after you left."

"And never came back," Carter growled.

"Right. The taxi was stolen from a car park in Shoreditch. They didn't even know it until we asked."

"Neat," Carter groaned, "very damn neat."

The Special Branch team was going over the flat like ants. One of the young officers answered Carter's questions as fast as he could ask them.

"The lady put up quite a struggle, sir. We found some blood. Won't know for a while yet whose it is."

"Any prints?"

"Lots, but that will also take a little time."

Carter lit a cigarette and cursed to himself, wondering if any of them would ever see Ravelle Dressler alive again.

The AXE safe house was an apartment in Kensington near Knightsbridge. It overlooked Hyde Park, and that was what Carter was looking at as he sipped a scotch and tried to figure.

The apartment had yielded nothing, nor had the interrogation in the surrounding streets. For the past thirty hours, Carter and a selected group from Special Branch and Scotland Yard had combed the dives from Southwark to Primrose Hill. Carter had tried everything from verbal intimidation to plain fist work, and it had yielded nothing.

Now, with night descending over Hyde Park, he was guessing that it was useless. El Adwan had won again. This time Ravelle Dressler had been the victim, and Carter blamed himself.

He reached across the bottle and small bucket of ice

for the phone. A special number had been set up to coordinate the search. It answered on the first ring.

"This is Carter. Anything?"

"Afraid not, sir, nothing new."

"Nothing on how they got her out of the building?"

"No, sir."

Carter groaned. "I'm going to grab a few hours of shut-eye. Call me if there's anything new . . . *anything!*"

"Yes, sir."

Carter hung up and refilled his glass. It was hot, muggy, oppressive, and breathless. The park was dark and ominous under a sky without stars. Somewhere above, rain loomed in gloomy clouds.

Where was she? And, wherever she was, was she still breathing?

Ravelle's face was numb from the beating. Her eyes were mere slits, practically swollen shut.

They were dragging her over slick grass, past trees into a thicker grove of trees. She tried to hold back, to set her heels, but they kept slipping, and the strength of the men moved her with comparative ease.

It was starting to rain. Her feet were wet and her hair was plastered to her head. Water ran down her neck, soaking her torn sweater.

She was still twisting and fighting when they came to a stop. She was twisted roughly so that she faced a spot where one of them beamed a flash.

"No! Oh, God, *no!*" she cried.

There was a grave. She was standing on the lip of a ready-dug grave. Beside it dirt was mounded, ready to go back into the hole.

Breath gone, unable now to scream, she watched as

the one called Horst played the light back and forth. At the bottom of the grave was a box. Inside rested a Thermos and wrapped sandwiches. A slender lead pipe extended to the surface.

Ravelle felt her knees buckle beneath her.

They were going to bury her alive.

Carter finished his drink and entered the flat, closing the balcony doors behind him. Something—a little man with an idea hammer—was pounding inside his head, but the message wouldn't come through.

He was hot and sweaty and wanted a shower. He lifted the phone, upped the bell's volume, and went into the bathroom. He looked at his face in the mirror, grimaced, and broke out his razor and lather. Finished shaving, he looked again in the mirror, and still grimaced.

He finished undressing and slipped under the sharp needle spray of the shower. It was cold and he left it that way.

Slowly his head cleared. Logic started to push aside the weariness in his brain. As the water rinsed the soap from his body, a new idea hit him.

Suddenly he knew.

He leaped from the tub and grabbed a towel. Briskly he dried himself as he ran to the phone, fidgeting impatiently until the officer picked up on the other end.

"Yeah, Carter again. Is Dakin still there?"

"I believe he's just leaving . . ."

"Catch him! This is an emergency!"

"Yes, sir!"

It was a full five minutes before Claude Dakin came on the line. "Yes, Nick, I was in my car. What is it?"

"Zev Rosenbaum's flat in Mayfair, just below Ravelle's . . ."

"What about it?"

"Has it been sealed since Rosenbaum was broiled in his shower?"

"Of course."

"And that tunnel El Adwan made between the walls . . . was it boarded back up?"

"Yes," Dakin replied, and then paused. "Nick, could they have . . ."

"Meet me there in twenty minutes!"

Carter quickly slammed down the phone and dressed. Five minutes later he was hailing a cab on Kensington Road.

Claude Dakin, looking alert and sharp even though Carter knew he had been up for as many hours as he had, waited with the doorman.

"Keys?" Carter asked.

"And combination," Dakin nodded.

"Let's go."

They had no need for the combination. The sealed master lock it fitted had been gutted from behind and resealed. Tiny scratches around the door lock itself told Carter that it had been picked.

They went in with their guns drawn, but there was no need. The apartment was as quiet as a tomb and just as musty. Carter stopped in the foyer, his nose alert.

"Smell it?"

"Perfume."

"Hers?" Dakin asked.

"Yeah."

Carter snapped on the light. A typewriter sat in the middle of the living room floor, a white sheet of paper gleaming in the carriage.

"Now, that takes balls," Dakin growled as they leaned over the machine.

CARTER.

IF YOU'RE READING THIS, YOUR POWERS
OF LOGIC ARE AS GOOD AS I ASSUMED.

THE WOMAN MEANS NOTHING TO ME. SHE
IS ALIVE AND SHE WILL STAY THAT WAY AS
LONG AS YOU COOPERATE.

IT'S YOU THAT I WANT.

IF YOU WANT TO GAMBLE FOR HER, PUT
AN AD IN THE EVENING STANDARD:
"ADELE—WILL MEET YOU HALFWAY—CALL
(WHATEVER NUMBER YOU CHOOSE)."

It wasn't signed.

"At least," Carter hissed, "there's a good chance the
bastard is keeping her alive."

ELEVEN

Jonathan Hart-Davis and Ernie Nevers shook hands with Sir Charles Dunwood and thanked him for the information. They were standing on Grosvenor Road outside the club where they had just lunched.

It was Monday, just after three o'clock.

As soon as Dunwood was in his car, the other two men began to walk.

"What do you think?" asked Nevers.

Jonathan Hart-Davis, walking slightly bent forward as if he were heading into a heavy gale, shrugged his shoulders. "Hard to say. With El Adwan here in London, I'd have to doubt if his dealings with Estes had anything to do with this supertanker *Thor 1*."

"True," Nevers replied, "but there are coincidences. I think we should have Carter at least talk to this Reed woman."

"Ernie, this is Lloyd's problem, whatever it is, and if we get involved, we're overstepping the bounds of MI6 and the Home Office. Also, Hannibal St. James has some very powerful friends."

"But what if Sir Charles's theories are true? Good God, sinking a supertanker?"

"What if they are?" Hart-Davis shrugged. "Insurance fraud, no matter how immense, is not exactly our province. What time is it?"

Nevers glanced at his wrist. "After three."

"The *Evening Standard* will be out."

They stopped at a newspaper stand by St. George's Hospital and bought a paper. Quickly, Hart-Davis turned to the personals column.

"It's in there. Thank God for that."

"Yes," Nevers replied, "but it is odd."

"What?"

"That they would choose the *Evening Standard*. We could have gotten the ad in any other paper on Saturday or Sunday. Why did they choose a paper that would not be out until Monday, three days after the woman was abducted?"

Hart-Davis tucked the paper under his arm and sucked on his unlit pipe. "No more odd than them assuming that Carter would think of Rosenbaum's flat. It might have been days before we realized they kept her there, right in the bulding, and took her out when we weren't covering it."

"All the same," Nevers mused, "if El Adwan wants a showdown with Carter, it seems to me that he wouldn't give us so much time to set up our defenses."

"Yes, it is odd. But everything the bloody bastard dreams up is odd!"

The two men parted, each going to respective offices. El Adwan was still their concern. They could do little about Ravelle Dressler. Her abduction was now in the hands of Special Branch, Scotland Yard, and Nick Carter.

The same questions asked by Ernie Nevers of the Home Office were going through Nick Carter's mind as he sat by a phone in the Whitehall offices of the Special Branch.

If El Adwan had assumed that Carter would think of the Rosenbaum flat, why arrange to take so long to get the ball rolling?

It didn't make sense.

He checked the wall clock: almost five. The *Standard* had been on the streets since two. Surely they would have seen the ad by now.

He crossed to a hot plate and was about to pour his twentieth cup of coffee of the day, when the phone rang. He grabbed it and remained silent until he heard the recorder and tracing devices click in.

"Yes?"

"Carter?"

"Yes."

"I will speak, you will listen. You have fifteen minutes to reach Victoria Station, main-floor bank of phones just inside the Palace Road entrance. Go now."

"What the hell do you want?" Carter growled, but the phone was already dead.

Claude Dakin met him at the door. "Car and driver waiting outside. This is typical. God knows where they'll run you around to."

Carter nodded. "Get a voiceprint on that. I'll call in."

The driver was good. Carter entered Victoria Station with two minutes to spare, and found the phones. Thankfully, none of them was in use.

On the minute, one of them rang.

"Carter here."

"You are very prompt. Are you alone?"

"I have a driver."

"Get rid of him. And make sure that no Yard cars or anyone else follows you."

"Where to now?" Carter said, gritting his teeth.

The words brought a laugh. "I see you know the routine."

"He wants me. Where is he? I'll meet him."

"In time. Drive to the British Airways Western Terminal on Cromwall Road. There are three phones near the car rental counters. You have eighteen minutes."

Carter dismissed the driver, who merely shrugged and handed him the keys. Carter knew London, so he was able to avoid traffic on the main streets. At the terminal he parked in an employee zone and dashed in with three minutes to spare. He used them to call Dakin.

"You're right, they're running me around. But for the life of me I can't figure out why."

"My guess is they want to get you in the open."

"Could be," Carter replied, "but that's the chance I have to take. What about the voiceprint?"

"Definitely German. He makes a good try at American English, but our man places him in Bavaria, probably around Munich."

"Good enough. I'll stay in touch."

A second phone nearby rang the moment he hung up.

"You're doing fine so far, Carter. Just keep doing it.

Do you know the village of Chagford, on the northern end of Dartmoor?"

"I know it."

"There is a hotel, the Mill End. Check in there tomorrow night, not before seven."

"Tomorrow night? For chrissake . . ."

"Bring a half million pounds. I understand the Dressler woman is worth far more than that."

"I thought it was *me* El Adwan wanted."

"It is, but we are the help in this operation. We have to be paid."

"If all this has to wait for tomorrow night, why the runaround today?"

"Just testing you, Carter, just testing you."

"Is Ravelle alive?"

"Very much alive."

"I want to talk to her," Carter growled.

"You will . . . soon."

The line went dead and Carter slammed the receiver down so hard that it cracked in half.

The restaurant was dim and smoky and the booze was expensive. It fit Carter's mood. Across from the Killmaster in a rear booth, Claude Dakin toyed with a pint of lager.

"You're right, Nick, it doesn't make sense. Why tomorrow night, and why Dartmoor? It doesn't figure."

"Not when the moor is wide open and can be covered from the air with choppers directed by me with a wire. No, I think I'll get directions to come right back here, or go somewhere else where I wait some more."

He paused, lit a cigarette, and sipped his own beer. Suddenly he looked up.

"Time."

"What?" Dakin asked.

"They're buying time. It's obvious. But what the hell for?"

"Search me. Does this mean you're not going to Chagford tomorrow night?"

"Oh, I'll go. I've got no choice. What about the money?"

"No problem," Dakin replied. "It will be ready."

"Anything on the German?"

"Nothing yet. Why don't you go back to the flat, get some rest?"

"You're right."

Carter pushed himself from the table and bid Claude Dakin good night. He drove to the AXE safe house and dialed Jonathan Hart-Davis before turning in.

"Anything from your people on El Adwan?"

"Nothing on him personally, but we know he was active in the Rome area up until a few days ago."

"What about MI5 here? Have they turned up anything?"

"Nothing, Nick, sorry."

Carter brought the MI6 man up to date on the Dressler situation, and hung up.

Jonathan Hart-Davis also hung up, and then thought of calling Carter right back and telling him about the lunch with Sir Charles Dunwood of Lloyd's. His hand was on the phone before he thought better of it.

Carter already had enough on his mind.

On the other side of London, Ernie Nevers was also thinking about the luncheon with Sir Charles. He had just finished a detailed memo of the entire conversation, and now he really didn't know where the copies should go.

Finally he made a list and dropped it on his secretary's desk to be copied and sent out.

The last name on the list was Nick Carter.

In Southwark, Horst Layman was drunk and on the prowl. Tomorrow night Carter would find the woman, and both of them would be dead. He hoped there would be no publicity about the money. That was his idea, and Mr. St. James would be very angry if he knew that his hired killer had deviated from the plan and tried to line his own pockets.

It was that guilt, borne out of fear of Hannibal St. James, that had made Horst Layman go on the prowl.

And it was turning out to be a lousy prowl.

He had been going from hotel lounge to hotel lounge and pub to pub for the last two hours, and found nothing. The ones who took in his ugly face and immense size and who were still willing were ugly themselves. The pretty ones were occupied. With each stop, he was consuming more liquor and losing just a little bit more of his mind.

Finally, in disgust, he hailed a cab and told the driver to cross back over the Thames.

"Where to?"

"Just drive."

The driver drove, aimlessly north, then west, then north again.

"Albany, across from Regent's Park."

Only about two miles from his Somerstown flat off Euston Road. Not far, but far enough.

"Stop here."

The driver stopped and took off again, quickly, as soon as he was paid. The giant with no neck and the heavy accent scared the hell out of him.

Layman tried the streetwalkers in the park. No good, and as he lumbered along sipping from the pint in his pocket, he got more depressed.

Half a million pounds. Even Hannibal St. James couldn't find him with half a million pounds.

Or could he? The old man wasn't what he used to be, especially now with Oliver Estes dead. But still . . .

He was propositioned time after time, but they weren't right. Each one that hit on him was wise-eyed, brazen, and cheap. Most of them probably had tracks on their arms and knives in their purses, or a pimp with a gun in the closet at their flat.

Not that Horst Layman couldn't handle either one. He had, many times, in the past.

The pint was gone. He saw a private club sign and staggered across the street. The lights were on inside and the place was empty.

"Sorry, sir, members only, and we're about to close."

"I just joined," Layman said, sliding a fifty-pound note across the bar.

The bill disappeared. "What will it be?"

"Whisky, soda, tall . . . no ice."

The drink materialized and Layman sipped it as he glanced toward the booths in the rear. He saw a waiter in a far corner, the usual somnambulant type who probably worked a regular shift somewhere else and then a couple of nights in an after-hours place to pay off a mortgage and raise four brats.

And then he saw her. She was the only other customer, alone in the far rear booth.

Her shoulder-length hair was so blond and glossy it looked as if sunlight was shining on it. Her skin was the color of a ripe peach, and her eyes were a deep blue. A heavy fringe of eyelashes cast feathery shadows across sculpted cheeks.

Horst Layman was interested.

And then, as though she knew she was being observed, she stood up. Her figure was fantastic in a tight-fitting jump suit with four slanting pockets. Her shoulder bag was white leather, matching a wide leather belt that encircled her small waist.

She was not only beautiful, she had class. And Horst Layman, watching her move, had a gut feeling.

"Know the lady?" he asked the bartender.

The man's gaze was opaque as he gazed through Layman. The big man laid a twenty on the bar.

"That's for the drink. The change joins the fifty."

"Thank you," said the bartender.

"So?"

"Never saw her before."

"C'mon."

"Serious. She's been there all night. Says she's waiting for a friend."

The woman returned from the rest room and slid back into the booth.

"What is she drinking?"

"Gin, tonic."

"Give me one, and another whiskey."

Layman took the drinks to the rear and slid in opposite the woman. Up close she was older but still as beautiful.

"You are a very beautiful woman. I could not resist buying you a drink. May I sit?"

"You already are." She smiled.

"I saw you go the ladies', and the strangest thought struck me."

"Oh?" she replied, folding long fingers over her glass.

"Yes. I thought that a woman with your class and beauty must have a rich husband, a rich lover, or a lucrative business for herself."

The smile faded, the eyebrow went down, and the

forehead furrowed. "Are you a policeman?"

"Me? I am German. How could I be an English police-man?"

"A point."

"Shall we talk essentials?"

"By essentials . . . ?" she said, leaning forward.

They were interrupted by the sleepy-eyed waiter. "Something?"

"Go away," Layman growled. The waiter moved, fast, and the big man turned his attention back to her, grinning. "My name is Gerhard."

"My name is Hilda."

"Hilda?"

Now the smile came back, wide. "You are German, tonight I am Hilda."

It was what Layman had been waiting to hear. "Why have you sat here all night, wasting your time?"

She shrugged. "A short story. I thought it was going to have an unhappy ending, but maybe it won't. My friend asked me to meet him here, but no-show." She looked at her watch. "And if he hasn't shown by now . . ."

"Nobody would stand *you* up."

"He's a married man. Married men can get hung up."

"So why didn't he call?"

"Maybe he can't get detached from the wife."

Layman drank. "You suggested the story could have a happy ending . . ."

Blue eyes slitted. "Depends on you, Gerhard."

"I get it." He grinned. "And you got it."

"Not so fast, my friend. I like to know what I'm doing."

"You know what you're doing."

"But it could be," she said, "that you don't. I'm very expensive. I'm not a street hooker. Not at all. Nothing

like that. I give of my time, but to a very select clientele."
She smiled demurely. "I took a chance on you. Intuition.
No, that's not quite true. I noticed you were very liberal
with the bartender. That makes you, kind of, my kind
of people."

"How much?" he said.

"Two hundred pounds. Not one-ninety-nine. Two
hundred." Now her smile was wide. "And I'll even cook
you bacon and eggs in the morning. Now look," she said,
"if it happens you don't have it on you, I don't accept
credit cards. We'll make it some other evening."

"Excuse me."

Layman went to the men's room and folded together
two hundred pounds. He returned to the booth and slid
the money into her palm.

"Excuse me," she said, and went to the ladies' room.

The bitch is counting my money, he thought. *Women!
The fucking bitches!* He drank down his whiskey.

She came back, the gorgeous hips swaying in the jump
suit, and eased into the booth.

"Shall we go?"

He shook his head. "You go, I follow. I have a wife."
He shrugged. "I'll meet you on the corner."

"How do you know I'll be there?"

"Because there is another hundred if you are. I think
you are greedy."

"You're so right," she said, smiling. "See you."

Layman watched the movement under the jump suit
all the way out the door, and took ten minutes to finish
his drink.

"No luck?" the bartender said as Layman passed.

"None. It's not my night."

• • •

"No cab," Horst Layman said.

They walked. She lived in a small building on Harley Street south of the park. It was perfect, two flats to a floor and no doorman.

"I'll just slip into something more comfortable."

"Don't bother," Layman said, lifting a bottle from a sideboard and drinking from it. He ran his tongue over his lips, his eyes never leaving her body.

"Hey, look, we've got all night. There's no hurry."

"That's just it. I want to use all night."

A tiny ripple of fear went up her spine. He had been big and ugly in the restaurant, but there had been nothing dangerous in him. Now his eyes had changed; they had an odd, almost demented look.

He moved close to her until she could smell the heavy reek of whiskey on his breath. He reached out until his fingertips touched the thin fabric covering her breasts.

Suddenly his powerful fingers curled the jump suit at her throat and shredded it to her navel.

She wore no bra, and Layman sucked in his breath as his eyes grew more demented gazing at her full, perfectly formed breasts.

The areolas stood out in harsh relief against the smooth contours of her flesh. Using his forefinger, he touched each nipple in turn. Then he drew an imaginary circle around each one. It was as if he were decorating them with a long-forgotten fertility rite. Reaching behind him, he swung a lamp around so that the light illuminated the objects of his intense interest.

"Take it off." The nostrils in his flat nose were flaring and the pupils of his eyes were all but gone.

"Hey, look, I may be a whore, but . . ."

With a roar he shoved the jump suit to her ankles and

then lifted her out of it, high into the air, before throwing her to the floor.

"Look, you son of a bitch . . ."

"You have a whip?"

"A *what*?" she gasped, feeling real fear now.

"A whip, get it!" he sneered, again at the bar drinking from the bottle.

"No, no, I don't go in for that . . ."

"Hah! A two-hundred-pounds-a-night hooker? You must have some kinky customers. Don't tell me you don't. Get it!"

"All right, all right, I'll get it." She crawled, naked, on all fours across the room to a lowboy. She opened the drawer, reached both arms in, and was halfway back out before Layman felt alarm.

He saw the gun, a tiny chrome .22, coming up in both hands, and lunged just as she fired.

Both slugs hit him in the middle of the stomach. A third one got him in the chest as he got his hands on her throat.

He turned to the side, trying to butt the gun from her hands. He succeeded, but not before she fired twice more. One slug caught him in the hip, the other entered his left side.

He howled in pain and butted his head into her face. At the same time, he yanked forward with his powerful hands.

It worked.

Her neck snapped like a twig.

Gasping, Laymen dropped her body. "Bitch! Bloody whore bitch!" he cried, and staggered toward a mirror.

Holes, the bitch had put holes all over his body and he was bleeding like a stuck pig!

A .22, he thought, *a woman's gun!*

But the holes were making him weak.

My flat, have to get back to my flat. . . .

But halfway to the door he knew he wouldn't make it.

Turning in mid-stride, he fell across a sofa and brought the telephone to the floor with him.

TWELVE

Rosario Duncan batted the covers away and sat up, bathed in sweat, at the first sound of the telephone. With sleep still filling his eyes, he groped with both hands until he found the hated instrument.

"Yes, yes, what is it?"

"Rosario, this is Horst."

"Jesus, it's four in the morning! I am not supposed to meet you until nine."

"Shut up. I need you."

"Now?"

"Now, you little Irish-Jamaican shit. Now listen, I am at Four-forty Harley, off Regent Park Circle."

"Christ, that's clear across—"

"Shut up!" Layman yelled, and then broke into a fit of coughing.

"Hey, man, you sound bad. What's the matter?"

"Shot, I've been shot. I want you to take me to a doctor I know in Paddington who won't ask questions. You got the address, Harley Street?"

"Yeah, I got it."

"Flat Five-B, top. Move your ass!"

Rosario Duncan cursed his drunken Irish father—and his Jamaican mother for giving up her lucrative whorehouse to marry him—as he shook himself into his clothes. Because of the poverty they had passed to him, he had to get up at four in the morning and go to the aid of a man he hated but depended upon.

Five minutes later he was in a battered Mini on the Lambeth Road heading across the Thames. He turned north, got through Whitehall, and the proceeded to get lost in the better section around Mayfair.

Other than doing an occasional job of villainy for people like Horst Layman—and a little housebreaking on his own—Duncan was rarely north of the Thames.

It took him a full hour to find Harley Street. He passed number 440 and parked a block away.

At the door of 5B he fretted over knocking. Shot, Layman had said. Was the shooter still around?

Finally he tried the knob. It turned, and Rosario Duncan walked into a nightmare.

He had heard rumors about Horst Layman's weird pastimes. Now he knew they were true.

Layman was just a few feet inside the door. It was obvious that he had staggered to the door, unlocked it, staggered back a few steps, and died.

The woman was also dead, her head at a crazy angle to her body.

Rosario Duncan didn't have to be a cop or a genius to figure out what had happened.

He stood in the center of the room and ground his knuckles into his cheeks. If Duncan had ever been capable of crying, it was now. "Shit, shit, shit, what do I do now?"

The dead mountain of flesh on the floor represented fifty thousand pounds to Duncan. That would be his cut of the payoff for snatching the Dressler woman.

He sank to his knees and beat at his temples, trying to think.

The woman was still in the grave. Should he call the police? But what about the money he had worked for?

Fifty thousand pounds.

But if his cut was fifty, Layman's was probably two, maybe three times that much.

The list. He had seen Layman refer to it for the phone numbers when they had run the American around to see what he looked like.

Gingerly, keeping his hands free from the blood, Duncan rolled the big body over. He found a wallet. Four hundred pounds. He pocketed that, and another hundred in small bills from a side pocket. He found the three pages in Layman's inside coat pocket.

It wasn't just a list of telephone numbers. It was the whole plan, written out in Layman's precise scrawl.

"Just like the bloody Germans," Duncan growled, "got to have it all down so they can remember it."

Rosario Duncan's dark face began to flush and the bile began to boil in his stomach as he read the detailed plan as set forth by the dead hulk at his feet.

By the time he had finished, he was kicking Horst Layman's inert form.

"You bastard, you bloody bastard! Setting me up for the fall, were you! I'm dead and you're bloody well free with the money, huh? Well, we'll see . . . we'll just see about that!"

But Rosario Duncan didn't see. He had the master plan as laid out by Layman, but it required two people.

How, he wondered, could he pull it off by himself?

For the moment it was too much for his small brain. Not one to miss the obvious, Duncan went through the apartment. He found seven hundred pounds in cash in the woman's closet, and pocketed the jewelry that was worth filching.

It was dawn when he slipped from the apartment and the building and drove back to his own grubby flat in Southwark.

An hour later, agonizing over a cup of coffee, he figured out an alternate to Layman's plan, an alternate that he could pull off by himself.

There was only one problem. Nothing in Layman's notes told him how to defuse the bloody bomb.

No matter. Let the sod who dug her up worry about that, or go up with her.

The alarm went off at six. Carter was up, showered, shaved, and dressed by six-thirty.

Outside, the rain was really lashing now, so thick that it was difficult to see the trees in the park. It was all set. He would drive to Chagford this morning and kill time moving around the area until it was time to check into the hotel.

He was pouring a second cup of coffee when the phone jarred him.

"Yeah?"

"Nick, Claude Dakin. Get down here right away."

"What's up?"

"Another phone call, evidently with new instructions. He just called—says he'll talk only to you. He'll call back at eight."

"Was it the German?"

"Afraid not, Nick. A new voice.'.'

"Shit."

"My sentiments exactly. There's a car on the way to you right now."

"I'm moving."

He shrugged into a raincoat, slipped on a rainhat, and went out into a whipping storm of rain.

By now they had the routine down to a science. When the phone rang, Carter picked it up and everyone went into action. A few-second delay and Carter answered.

"This is Carter."

"The hotel in Chagford is off. You still head for Dartmoor, but you do it now. This rain is heading west."

"Rain?" Carter growled. "What's the rain got to do with it?"

"If it rains down there, the bloody woman's going to drown."

"You son of a—"

"Save the names, mate. Here's the gaff. You come alone. You drive a blue and white London Yard car with the blue lights flashing all the time. From Reading on, you drive exactly sixty miles an hour. At Exeter, you take the A30 west. You got that?"

"I do. What about the money?"

"Comin' to that, mate. You get yerself a Colestar AV200 hand send/receive unit, and set it on channel four. You turn it on at Exeter. Now, the money. You divide it equally into three bank bags. Understand?"

"I don't get it. Why three—"

The voice suddenly went hysterical. "You don't have to get it, damn you! Just listen and do what I say!"

"All right, all right," Carter said. "The money goes in three bags."

"Right. All used fifties and hundreds, and if the numbers are consecutive, the show's over. Now listen, you bloody bastard, if there's a helicopter around, or a car tailing you, or one lousy transmission from the police radio in your car, or anything that I think smells like coppers, I'm gone and she's dead by remote control!"

"Just don't get nervous," Carter urged. "Now, where does El Adwan come into all this?"

"Adwan? Who the hell is Al Adwan?"

"*El* Adwan," Carter said, exchanging a cloudy look with Claude Dakin.

"I don't know anything about any El Adwan. Don't confuse me. Just do as you're told, mate!"

The line went dead. By the end of the conversation the man's voice had risen to an hysterical pitch.

"Little nervous, isn't he?" commented Dakin.

"More than that, he's scared to death," Carter replied.

"Definitely," said the voice man, removing the phones from his ears. "Lots of stress. I'd say he's a man on the edge."

"That might eventually work in our favor," Carter said. "What about the accent?"

"West Indies, but it's hard to pinpoint with the Cockney mixed in. But the singsong phrasing is there."

"Black?"

The man shrugged. "Fifty-fifty chance. There are whites in this country who grew up in Jamaica and came back with the accent."

"Sir . . ." It was the sector man sitting before a huge map of London. "The call came from section six, Lambeth. A pay phone."

"Figures," Carter said. "He'll be long gone by now."

"We'll have a Bentley, two Rollses, and four lorries moving around you all the time," Dakin said.

Carter nodded. "Have them stay clear until I hit Exeter. What the hell is a Colestar AV200?"

A voice from the rear of the room replied. "It's a powerful little devil, sir. It operates up to thirty miles, and on a high frequency that's almost impossible to pinpoint if he sends in short spurts."

Claude Dakin moved close to the Killmaster. "Are you thinking what I'm thinking about his comment?"

"You mean, she's dead by remote control?" Dakin nodded. "Have a bomb squad in the back of one of the lorries."

"And El Adwan?" Dakin added.

"I think the whole thing's a blind. Get in touch with Hart-Davis and have him put pressure on his people in Rome and the Near East. I don't think El Adwan's in London at all. But I do think he's behind this. It has his style."

"But why?"

"If we knew that," Carter said, "we'd already be two jumps ahead of him. As it is, Ravelle Dressler is the most important problem at the moment. We owe her."

"If she's still alive," Dakin murmured.

"Yeah. If she's still alive."

Carter's mind was a jumble as he headed for the underground garage.

He was to drive at precisely sixty miles an hour. Their man had called from south London. That meant he was buying time to get to the drop—or, in this case, drops—before Carter.

Three bags. That probably meant that the man would pick up only one of the bags, settling for a third of the loot, knowing that all three drops couldn't be covered. Especially when they were controlled by radio.

And where was the cool, calculating German?

This new one was obviously in over his head, and from the sudden change in plans, he was obviously improvising.

The Killmaster only hoped that would work in their favor.

And where the hell was Abu El Adwan?

THIRTEEN

He was four miles west of Exeter on the A30 when the unit on the seat beside him came to life.

"Carter, are you there?"

"I'm here," he replied, gritting his teeth at the cocky, singsong voice coming from the small speaker.

"All right, here's the gaff. The woman is in a grave. After the last drop, I tell you where. But that's not all. There's a pound of plastique under her, and the detonator is controlled by a radio device. You understand?"

"I do."

"You'd better, mate. After you make the last drop, I tell you where to go. When you get there, I tell you how to defuse the bomb. That is, I tell you *if* I don't have any problems. You know what I mean by problems?"

"I've got a pretty good idea."

"Good for you, mate. We'll be talking again."

From the roof of a telephone repairman's van, on a rise a quarter of a mile south of the A30, Rosario Duncan set the hand unit down and picked up a pair of powerful glasses.

He scanned the highway in front of Carter and as far as he could see behind him. He saw nothing suspicious, but that didn't mean they weren't there somewhere.

He chuckled nervously.

In Layman's original plan, it would have been Layman with the radio and the binoculars, while Duncan took the gamble of making the single pickup from a single drop. If the drop was safe, Layman would take the money and Duncan would direct Carter by radio.

Suicide.

When the bomb went, they would have been all over Duncan like flies on honey.

Well, not now. Now *he* was directing the whole operation.

He picked up the unit. "Carter?"

"Yeah."

"You're two miles past B3212."

"I know."

"Turn around and go back. Take B3212 to Morton Hampstead."

Duncan watched the flashing blue lights make a U-turn. When no vehicles made a U-turn behind, he climbed into the van.

In the back of a truck with COLLIER'S MEAT PIES emblazoned on its side, two men sat in front of a mass of electronic gear.

"Got that?"

"Yeah. Unit Two is at Morton just ahead of us. There's a country lane there that will take them south directly to Morton Hampstead."

"Send 'em." A chuckle. "A chauffeured Rolls on that road will blow the natives' minds."

"Carter?"

"Yes."

"You're coming up on a wide curve."

"I see it."

"Slow down . . . get one of the bags ready."

The Killmaster did as he was told, and rolled down the car window.

"All right, now—over the side with it!"

The bag sailed out the window and over the side. Carter saw it tumble down the bank and stop just short of a stream.

"Good show, mate. A mile on is the B3193. Take it back to the A30. And, Carter . . ."

"Yes."

"If I see so much as one car, she's dead."

And in the meat pie truck:

"Damn, the bastard has boozled us! There's no traffic for miles on that road. A unit would be spotted for sure!"

"Chopper?"

"Are you nuts? No, that one's lost."

"I can put a man in on foot."

"Try it, but tell him to go slow and stay under cover. If our boy is telling the truth, one man spotted and the woman goes boom."

"Carter, where are you?"

"Almost to the Tedburn St. Mary Road."

"Take it, north. Just inside the village there's a pub, The King's Arms."

"The pubs don't open until eleven."

"I know that!" Duncan screamed into the unit. "Drive around behind the pub. Drop the bag into the trash bin. Then go on north. Take the first lane west and head for Colebrooke."

"Damn you," Carter hissed, "that's taking me away from Chagford."

An almost hysterical laugh came through the unit. "Maybe she's not buried at Chagford!"

Carter found the pub and deposited the second bag.

Duncan was through playing cat and mouse now. No one had come near the bag on the B3212, at least on the road. There was a good chance, however, that they had someone coming at it on the ground.

No matter. They could have that one.

He cut off the A30 south and headed for the waste processing plant near the eastern edge of Dartmoor.

The chief engineer in the control truck marked Collier's Meat Pies carefully tuned the dials in front of him. "Odd."

"What?"

"Carter's signal is clear as a bell. The signal from the target unit is cutting out every now and then."

"Could it be because it's getting weaker?"

"No, I know the AV200. He also isn't clear. It's like there was something in the unit interfering with the connections, the wiring."

"Control, this is Unit Three."

"Unit Three, that's the Henkel's Auto Parts lorry. Tell him to go ahead."

"Got you, Unit Three."

"A garbage lorry is picking up the bin behind the pub."

"Get its number and keep them in sight, Unit Three. Unit Four?"

"Unit Four here."

"You're in the lumber lorry, right?"

"Right."

"Head for the landfill and the waste processing plant on the eastern side of Dartmoor. It's near Monaton."

"We're on the way."

"Carter, can you hear me?"

"Yes, but faintly."

"That's good enough. Pull over."

Carter wheeled to the side of the narrow lane and stopped. "All right, what now?"

"Leave the car running. Get out. Leave the third bag and take your unit. Head south on the Colebrooke Road until you hit the A30. When you get there, mate, call me."

The Killmaster cursed to himself and left the car. It would be at least a half-hour walk to the A30, and he knew the other units were farther away than that.

The target could be twenty miles north in the Scotland Yard car and switch to another vehicle before they would spot him.

That is, if it was the third bag he intended taking.

God, Carter thought, *what a mess.*

The two officers in the Collier's Meat Pie van were thinking the same thing. They sent the Bentley and the other Rolls north to try and spot the blue and white police car if he headed that way.

"God, the bugger has really spread us out."

"That was his intent, I'm sure."

• • •

Duncan pulled the telephone truck in behind the restaurant and climbed out. He was dressed in blue coveralls with a utility belt around his waist. In seconds he had strapped on a pair of climbing spurs and scaled a pole adjacent to the building.

From that vantage point, he could see the road in both directions for nearly three miles and every square inch of the parking lot.

Right now there were six of the big garbage trucks parked in front and to the side of the restaurant. Within a half hour there would be a dozen more.

"Control, this is Conroy. I'm on foot upstream from the B3212 drop. The bag is still there."

"Control, this is Unit Three. We're about four miles behind the garbage lorry, but it's hilly. He keeps dropping out of sight."

"Keep your position, Unit Three. We have Unit Four near the plant."

Duncan had to squint, but he could see the plate number on the side as the garbage truck pulled in: 921. The big vehicle pulled in at the end of the line. Now there were ten of them in the line.

The driver and his helper were barely in the restaurant before Duncan was down from his perch.

Walking with spread legs so he wouldn't gouge himself with the climbing spurs, he ran around the restaurant and between the trucks. He lifted the 921 plate from its drop-in slide and ran down the line. At truck number 826 he switched plates and ran back to the original 921 vehicle.

There he dropped the 826 plate, and headed back to his pole.

He was on top playing with a few wires when a small truck approached the restaurant and slowed. On its side was a socket wrench logo and the words HENKEL'S AUTO PARTS.

"Control, this is Unit Three."

"Go ahead."

"There's a little roadside restaurant about five miles from the processing plant. Looks like all the drivers stop there on the way in for lunch."

"Unit Three, can you spot your truck?"

"Pulling into the drive now . . . going down the line . . . got it, number nine-two-one."

"Good enough. You'd better go in . . . have a cup of tea or something. Stay inconspicuous."

"Righto."

Atop his pole, Duncan was chuckling to himself. He watched the auto parts truck stop and two men get out. As much as they tried, their eyes kept going to the 921 truck as they entered the restaurant.

"Got you," he said aloud, and leaned back in his safety belt to wait.

The Bentley, with Claude Dakin and a driver, met Carter about a mile north of the A30.

"What's the latest?" the Killmaster asked.

"Not good," the Special Branch man replied with a sigh, "at least so far. The bugger may be nervous, but he's cunning."

"How so?"

"He hasn't touched a single bag. We have a man on foot watching the first one. Nothing. It's still in the creek bed."

"Figures," Carter replied. "That area is open for us, but also for him, too. What about the trash bin behind the pub?"

"Two units—one on the lorry, the other waiting at the processing plant. He hasn't made a try."

"And the Scotland Yard car, with the third bag?"

"Ditto, Nick. The damn thing is sitting there with the motor running."

"Damn," Carter hissed, slamming the fist of one hand into the palm of the other, "what the hell is going on? First we get the German. His bag seemed to be a link to El Adwan wanting to get to me. Now we've got a Jamaican who seems to be only after the money."

The two men fell silent, and in the silence exchanged a haggard, knowing look. It was Claude Dakin who spoke first, voicing the thought on both their minds.

"Adwan set it up."

Carter nodded. "And he's off somewhere doing his thing. The key is the bomb, if there is one."

"My guess," Dakin replied, "is that there definitely is one—and you're not supposed to know about it."

The driver and helper of the newly christened 921 garbage truck emerged from the restaurant. The big truck had barely backed around and headed off when the two men belonging to the auto parts truck walked briskly across the parking lot and gave chase.

The whole thing brought a wide smile to Rosario Duncan's face. He had outfoxed them!

Down the pole he went. He threw the climbing spurs

into the rear of the telephone van and closed the doors. Then he ran around to the garbage truck marked 826 and climbed up into the rear of the cab. There he pulled a ski mask down over his face, and from insde his coveralls drew a big-bore Webley service revolver.

It didn't take long. The driver and helper climbed up into the cab. The engine had just caught when Duncan pressed the barrel of the Webley against the back of the driver's head.

"You do everything just as I say, mate, and yer gonna live to eat yer supper tonight."

"What the hell . . . ?"

"Rafe, he's got a bloody cannon!"

"Then I'll bloody well do what he wants me to."

"Good show, lads. Take the road back, away from the processing plant."

The driver did as he was told. Two miles back, he was instructed to turn off, down a small lane. Two miles farther, he was instructed to turn into an open field. A stream ran nearby through a thick grove of trees, and a herd of sheep grazed in the field.

"Very good, mate," Duncan said, handing the driver a thick roll of electrician's tape. "Now, tie up yer helper, and tie 'im tight."

"Sorry," the man murmured to his companion.

"Just do what he says, Rafe. If the bugger wants to steal garbage, let him have it."

When the helper was tied up, Duncan performed the same function on the driver. This done, he laid both men out on the ground on the far side of the truck, away from the trees and the stream.

It took him three tries before he found the right sequence to the hydraulic gears. When he did, and garbage began to spew from the back of the truck he eased it forward a few feet every few seconds to spread it out.

He spotted the bag at once, caught it up, and headed for the trees. Deep within their cover, he shed the coveralls. Beneath them he wore black cycle leathers. The big BMW that went with the leathers was hidden in a thick patch of greenery at the base of the trees.

Just before he tied the bag behind the saddle, he opened it.

Up to this point, Rosario Duncan had been fairly calm. Now, siphoning through the mound of bills in the bag, his hands began to shake.

"Gar, there must be over a hundred and fifty thousand quid! Layman, you thieving son of a bitch, you were gonna give me a lousy fifty thou. Well, up yours, you German prick!"

Rosario Duncan was laughing with glee as he kicked the BMW to life and roared out of the trees.

"This is Control calling Dakin. Are you there?"

Claude Dakin grabbed the hand-held microphone. "This is Dakin. Go ahead."

"Sir, Unit Three is at the processing plant. The garbage lorry has dumped its load on the conveyor belt. Sir, they want orders. If the bag is on that conveyor, it's on its way into the incinerator."

"Oh, Christ, what now?" Dakin hissed.

Carter made a lightning decision. "Stop it. Retrieve the bag. That's obviously not the one he's after."

"Control, Dakin here."

"Yes, sir?"

"Have them stop the belt and retrieve the bag. Keep up surveillance on bags one and three."

"Yes, sir."

The transmission was scarcely completed when the AV200 unit in Carter's hand came to life.

"Carter? Carter, are you there?"

"Yes, dammit, I'm here. What the hell is going on? We've done everything you asked . . ."

"Shut up. I'm gonna do you a big favor. I'm tellin' you where the woman is buried. Listen close, because I'm only gonna say it once. You ready?"

"I'm ready," Carter said, "but you've got a lot of background noise. Can you speak louder?"

"In the Teign forest, halfway between the A30 and A32. Got that?"

"Got it."

"There's an abandoned caretaker's cottage exactly three point two miles east of the Easton turnoff. It's on the river. Take three hundred paces south from the front door of the cottage. You'll see a pipe sticking out of the ground about a foot."

"What about the bomb?" Carter asked, his palms sweating.

"You'll get that information if there's no one on me when you get there."

The unit went dead.

"The bastard is covering his ass, isn't he?" Dakin rasped.

"He sure as hell is. Tell Control that he's probably on a motorcycle, but not to go near him if he's sighted. Now, let's find Ravelle!"

The rain had started, not hard, but hard enough to make their slickers gleam as they searched.

The thick clouds overhead had turned day into night. So much so that now they were using lanterns.

Carter, bent over, his eyes slitted against the rain,

shone his light everywhere—on undisturbed, rain-beaten grass, on trees, on every muddy depression in the soil— but they had circled the entire area and still found no pipe.

On he moved, sometimes in a crouch, shining his light, foot by foot, going ahead a few inches at a time, then sideways, laying out rough squares of area in his mind, covering every inch of every square.

Around him he could hear other men doing the same thing, and always, in the back of his mind, were the kidnapper's words: "If it rains down there, the bloody woman's going to drown."

He had to watch his feet, where he set them, because there was loose brush everywhere. He aimed the light under and around each bush. Nothing.

He went further to the left, covered sodden squares of growth. The trees thickened, slowed him more than he wanted to be slowed, but he held himself back, examining the trees, the bushes, the ground.

Ahead, the beam wavered over a collection of brush. It had drifted down from the trees so that it made a patch of brush much thicker than he'd seen yet.

A fist started in his belly. He didn't give a damn whether it hurt or not. His gut feeling was strong.

He went for that brush. No matter how useless, or what time it consumed, he had to make sure. He stood at one end of it, noted that it looked to be almost rectangular, and shone his light the length of it, walking slowly. The grass and pieces of bush and even a couple of smallish branches set his back hair stiff.

He studied how rain had flattened it all, how it was still flattening. He dropped to his knees, set the light down, felt along one side of the patch, and came on dirt. Loose, wet dirt.

The fist in his belly started pounding. He tore brush

and long pieces of loose grass and brush away, slinging them aside, and he saw bare dirt. And then, as he stripped away a clump of brush, he saw a pipe sticking up out of the ground.

He ripped away at the brush. Underneath was bare, packed earth the length and width of a grave. He dug his fingers into the middle and found looseness.

His heart was punching everywhere, even in his heels. His breath tore in and out of his lungs. He dug with fingernails and hands like a madman.

And then common sense and sanity returned. He put his lips to the pipe.

"Ravelle . . . Ravelle?"

His ear to the pipe. He heard a gasp. A sigh.

"Ravelle, it's Nick. Ravelle . . . ?"

"Yes . . . here . . ."

"Ravelle, we're going to dig you out. Don't move, and keep your eyes closed. Do you understand?"

"Yes . . . understand . . ."

"Over here!" Carter shouted. "I've found her!"

He reached for the Colestar unit and depressed the "send" button.

Rosario Duncan was sticking to the speed limit, even under it, staying on narrow country lanes practically hidden from view by hedgerows. He was heading north now, and would soon turn left and drop into Wales.

"This is Carter . . . are you there?"

Duncan idled down a little.

"This is Carter. Somehow you got your money. So be it. Now what about the bomb!"

"Damned if I know, mate," Duncan said to the wind, and shut the unit off.

• • •

Lydell Harmon wasn't a man who visually inspired confidence. He seemed to be constructed of all odds and ends of body parts. His chest and torso were broad, almost barrel-shaped. His waist was as big as his chest, and his hips as big as his waist. There was little grace about him, for his arms and legs appeared to move in opposition to his body.

But he was the best bomb man in England, according to Dakin, and he had taken over with a vengeance.

Now he approached Carter with a grim face.

"We're down to the lid of the box from the top," he growled in a no-nonsense voice. "We've also tunneled in from the side under the box."

"And?" Carter said.

"There's a bomb, all right, a bloody bad one with a tricky double detonator."

"So," Carter said, forcing his voice to remain calm, "what do we do?"

"I gather the target isn't living up to his part of the bargain?"

Carter shook his head. "He won't answer."

"Then we'll have to do it ourselves. There's a pressure pad directly under the woman. She's lifted up at all, takes her weight off the pad, and boom. Follow me."

Carter followed him over to the grave and gazed down. About two inches of dirt still covered the lid of the box. From a hole near the top at the break between top and sides, the pipe extended.

"She'll probably trust you more than anyone else," Harmon said. "You game?"

"Just tell me what you want me to do," Carter replied.

"Okay, you're going to be on top. I'll be below. Don't let her move as you lift the lid. Get into the box with her. Get your hands under the small of her back. As the lads pull her out, you keep the pad depressed. Got that?"

"Got it."

"When she's out, I'll disconnnect the wires to the trigger device on the pad. But that's not all."

"An alternate?"

Harmon nodded. "Our boy wasn't taking any chances. I'm going to rig a cut-around to the alternate with a long breaker wire. We can't stop the blow but we can delay it for maybe sixty seconds."

"Long enough for us to get the hell out of here."

"You got it, laddie," Harmon said. "And one more thing . . ."

"Yeah?"

"Your boy was lying to you."

"About what?" Carter asked.

"The unit on the bomb is not a receive unit. It's for send only."

"That means he couldn't blow the bomb by remote control . . ."

Harmon shook his head. "No way. When the boom goes, an impulse goes *out*, not in. You ready?"

"Why not," Carter growled, easing himself down in to the hole and leaning forward until his face was close to the lid.

"Ravelle . . . it's me, Nick."

"Yes."

"Can you hear me?"

"Yes." She sounded out of it.

"Ravelle, it won't be long now. You must do exactly as I say. You must not move when I lift the lid until I tell you to move. Do you understand?"

"What?"

Carter heard groans from the men at graveside above him, and wiped the sweat from his eyes.

Again, slowly, he repeated everything. This time he got an affirmative answer from her.

"All right, I'm going to dig the rest of the dirt from the lid and then lift it. Don't move, and keep your eyes closed. Are you ready?"

"Yes . . . I understand."

"Good girl."

Rain shrouded them now as Carter started to dig with his hands through the last layer. He tasted dirt and he got it in his eyes as he threw it over his shoulder.

Then, slowly, talking to her all the while, he lifted the lid.

She was on her back, her face turned to the side. The end of the pipe was in her mouth, and the water was eddying around her ears.

Good God, Carter thought, another half hour and she would have drowned.

"Don't move, baby. For God's sake, don't move."

He tugged at the pipe. She grabbed for it, tried to get it back into her mouth.

"No, Ravelle," he yelled, "quit fighting! You don't need it now!"

Miraculously, she did.

He moved down and slid his hands between her legs, then outward.

"Lift your legs . . . not your hips, your legs, hear me?"

Slowly, the legs came up and Carter slid his hands under the small of her back.

"Harmon?"

"I'm down here."

"I've got pressure on the pad."

"All right, lads, get her wrists and ankles and ease her up."

They did. Carter ducked his head, and Ravelle's body disappeared above him.

"Got her!" a voice called. "She's out!"

"Good show," Harmon said. "Now get clear yourselves, all of you!"

There was the slap of feet on soggy grass, and then deathly silence.

"You're doin' fine, lad," Harmon said to Carter. "Just get ready to dive out and run like hell when I give you the word."

"How do you know," Carter asked, "that the impulse sender unit isn't to detonate another bomb in the area?"

"I don't," Harmon chuckled. "But it looks to be set up on a high frequency. That would normally mean long range."

"I hope you guess right," Carter said, almost blind now with the sweat in his eyes.

"So do I. You ready?"

"Ready."

"Then go, laddie!"

Carter took a deep breath, lifted his hands from the pad, and leaped from the grave. He scrambled from his knees to his feet and, with Harmon right beside him, ran like hell.

They were nearly two hundred yards from the grave and the blast still knocked them off their feet.

Rosario Duncan barreled out of the small lane onto the A3072. In an hour he would be at Hartland Point. There he would hide until dark, when an obliging fisherman would, for five hundred quid, take him to Ireland.

Duncan had friends in Ireland who would hide him until all was quiet and another boat could smuggle him to France.

He had done it! He had gotten away with it and he was rich!

He was laughing wildly, rolling the throttle to full, when the Colestar AV200 unit on his belt began to heat up.

Inside it, a tiny wire from a microreceiver unit glowed red for only a millisecond, and then ignited the three ounces of plastique that had been layered into the unit.

It was not a huge explosion.

Just enought to cut Rosario Duncan in half.

FOURTEEN

At seven o'clock in the morning, the rains had stopped, the clouds had drifted away, and sunshine permeated the drawn blinds. Carter roused from his sleep and found himself in an armchair. He blinked sleep from his eyes and it wouldn't go away. Finally he oriented himself, and remembered.

A cleanup crew in the west, a chopper into London, Ravelle into the emergency ward, and Carter passing out on his feet from fatigue. A driver had brought him to the AXE flat where he had tried to make the bed, but had given up in the armchair without even removing his clothes.

His mouth felt like the Russian front and every bone in his body ached.

Hoisting himself with a graon, he stumbled to the bathroom. He gargled with some mouthwash, rinsed, and spat. Then he went back to the bedroom, trailing clothes behind him, and picked up the phone. The hospital number picked up at once.

"Special Ward, Sayers speaking."

"Miss Sayers, Nick Carter here. How's our patient?"

"Resting comfortably, sir."

"And the final diagnosis?"

"Shock, of course, and exposure. There were no internal injuries and her bruises weren't serious."

"Good. She isn't raving anymore?"

"No, sir. The sedative worked fine. She's sleeping well."

"Any prognosis on when we can get a statement?"

"I believe the doctor is going to let some chaps from your office talk to her this afternoon."

"Thanks." Carter hung up and dialed the hot line at Special Branch. "Carter here. Anything new?"

"The motorcyclist was definitely our man. Got an ID on him, one Rosario Duncan, small-time hood, minor record."

"Nothing on the German?"

"No, sir, not yet."

"Please call me at one o'clock," Carter said. "And let the phone ring until I answer."

"Will do, sir."

"Thank you."

He went to the bed, slid into the cool, clean sheets, and slept until the ringing of the phone woke him.

It was Ernie Nevers from the Home Office. "I'm making your wake-up call myself to apologize."

"Oh?"

"Yes, for not reading between the lines. I think we've had some wires crossed on communications between agencies, Nick. But they're uncrossed now. We're finally pooling information again, and it's hot. We're all meeting with Hart-Davis in Whitehall at three."

"I'll be there."

Carter went over the statement that had been taken an hour earlier from Ravelle Dressler:

". . . And twice I heard him on the phone to someone who must have been his superior . . . and twice he assured the person that the timing would be perfect, the ship would be loaded and back at sea before any authorities caught on . . . he stressed this . . ."

Carter set the statement down and picked up the Scotland Yard report on a double homicide. He scanned it, set it aside, and looked up at the men assembled around the conference table.

"What about the woman?" he asked.

"A free-lance prostitute. Horst Layman had a background of abusing women. He was indicted twice for it in Germany, but never convicted. Mrs. Dressler's description of the two men fit Layman and Duncan perfectly."

"Okay," Carter sighed, "*that* mystery is solved."

Jonathan Hart-Davis nodded. "And it looks like the mystery of *why* is solved as well, Nick. I'm just sorry we didn't put it all together right from the moment the woman was kidnapped. Now it all fits."

Carter grunted his agreement. "El Adwan wanted me out of the way, and he wanted to stall all of us until he makes a try for this supertanker, the *Thor I*."

Avery Hopkins, head of the International Maritime

Commission, spoke up. "The problem, as I see it, is time. Is this terrorist, El Adwan, and his lot already on the ship? And if he is, what will his demands be?"

Carter thought on this for a moment before he replied. "I think it's back to the source. There is little doubt now, with the connection of Oliver Estes and Horst Layman to both Abu El Adwan and Hannibal St. James, that St. James is behind this. My fear is El Adwan. Is he doing this just for money? Or does he have a dual purpose?"

"Such as . . . ?" Hart-Davis asked.

"El Adwan," Carter said, "is a supreme egotist. Scuttling the *Thor I* for money would be one thing. But scuttling the ship for profit while building his owns stock as a man who will do anything would be an added plus. I think we must go to Hannibal St. James himself and get the original plan before we can guess how El Adwan will deviate from it."

There was a general chorus of groans around the table, until the Lloyd's representative, Sir Charles Dunwood, spoke up.

"I'm inclined to agree with Mr. Carter."

"All well and good," said Ernie Nevers, "but everything we have is circumstantial. It all links to St. James, but it may take months to prove it. And months we don't have."

"Then we bluff," Carter said. "Bluff and intimidate."

"Nick," Nevers replied, "we can't—"

"*You* can't," Carter growled, "but I can. Sir Charles . . ."

"Yes?"

"How good is this Carolyn Reed?"

"The best. She is a graduate maritime engineer. For the past several years her specialty has been these behemoth tankers."

"Good. I'll be in touch with her after St. James. Where is the *Thor I* now?"

Sir Charles Dunwood replied. "In the Persian Gulf, off Kuwait. She took on provisions and topped her own fuel tanks during the night."

"And the crude?" Carter asked.

Dunwood looked at his watch. "They should start loading about five our time."

"Jonathan," Carter said, turning to Hart-Davis, "can you get to the Kuwaitis?"

"I'm sure the P.M. can."

"Then do it, and very quietly. Instead of crude in those tanks when the *Thor I* sails, I want water in them."

"I suppose that can be done," Hart-Davis replied. "But why don't we just give a stop-sail order?"

"Because," Carter said, "if El Adwan is already on the ship, I don't think he'll hesitate to blow it right there. How many officers and crewmen are on board?"

Sir Charles did a quick shuffle of papers in front of him. "One hundred and eighty-six."

" 'Nuf said," Carter replied. "I assume Horst Layman's flat has been searched?"

"Stripped," Claude Dakin said.

"All right," Carter said, "I'll need a top-notch stenographer and your best forger. Let's get to work!"

No pier or harbor in the world was large enough to handle the *Thor I*. For this reason, the behemoth tanker was anchored a half mile from the main port of Al Kuwait in the Persian Gulf.

Captain Alonso Wakefield stood at the front of the bridge and watched the last of the huge foodstuff containers being craned down into the hold. Halfway between the ship and land he could see two tugs making for the

Thor I. Between them they carried the huge tube that would soon be pumping a million barrels of crude into the tanks of the ship.

The first officer stepped onto the bridge and smartly saluted the skipper. "Foodstuff containers all on board, sir, and our tanks are topped off."

"Good, Mr. Richardson. How soon can we start pumping?"

"About an hour, sir."

"Excellent. Tell the lads to step lively. And for God's sake, make sure there are no mistakes on the hookup."

"Yes, sir."

Jordon Conover was the head engineer for all pumping operations at the huge port of Al Kuwait. He was British, and employed by the Kuwaiti government. This evening he would supervise the biggest operation of his life and the first of its kind in the world.

He parked his car and craned his neck to see the huge tanker offshore as he walked toward his office.

"Good afternoon."

"Good afternoon, sir," replied his secretary, and handed him a stack of messages.

"Get me Obar on the phone right away."

"Yes, sir."

Conover laid the messages on the desk. He removed his jacket and hung it on the back of his swivel chair. He pulled down his tie, opened his shirt collar, and sat down in his swivel chair just as the phone rang.

"Hello, boss."

"Obar, how are we doing?"

"They are sleeving up the cord now. We're running a little behind schedule. Should be ready to pump in about an hour."

"Good," Conover said, rising and pacing in front of the big window that overlooked the enormous white tanks that swallowed and stored the crude as it poured in from the far desert. "Don't move a valve until I get there. I want to check everything one time myself."

"Will do, boss."

Conover hung up just as a long Mercedes limousine pulled up below his office window. The rear door was opened and a white-robed figure emerged and hurried into the building.

"My God," Conover said aloud, "what the hell is he doing here?"

He met his visitor at the door and bowed him into the office.

"Your Excellency, I'm surprised, to say the least. Please, sir, sit down."

"There is no time for amenities, Mr. Conover," the dark-skinned man replied in precise Cambridge English. "I have a request that we must discuss at once."

For the next ten minutes, Jordan Conover stood, his arms at his sides and his jaw agape, as his visitor spoke.

"Can this be done, Mr. Conover?"

"Yes, Your Excellency, it can be done. But may I ask why?"

"No, not at the present time."

"Let me understand this completely. You want me to fill the *Thor I*'s cargo tanks with seawater?"

"That is correct, Mr. Conover. And I want the fewest possible workmen to know about it."

"You realize, sir, that the expense will be enormous?"

The man smiled. "The expense will be far greater if anyone on the *Thor I* discovers what you are doing, Mr. Conover. See that they don't."

●   ●   ●

When someone is killed on your very doorstep, the best place to be at the time of the murder is somewhere else, surrounded by witnesses . . . as many as possible. This especially holds true if you are responsible for ordering the execution in the first place. Surrounded by witnesses, and with trusted people carrying out the actual killing, you have an established alibi hard to ignore in court.

It's a matter of common sense, and one that Hannibal St. James adhered to in all things.

That was why, immediately after ordering Horst Layman on his errand and being reasonably sure that El Adwan was in place for the hijacking of the *Thor I,* Hannibal St. James had departed his immense estate in Surrey. He had come by helicopter to his almost equally lavish estate on the cliffs above Lyme Regis in the south of England.

In his party were a film director and his wife, an aging star, two executives from a French auto company who wanted St. James to buy their failing company, and various minor officials of his subsidiary companies and their wives.

In such company he was safe and he had an alibi. That was why, on this balmy afternoon, he felt at ease and at peace with the world as he stood in his third-floor bedroom and watched his guests frolic by the pool below.

"Mr. St. James? Hannibal St. James?"

St. James whirled. The man was big, well over six feet, with black hair, a granite face, and piercing eyes. He was dressed in a pair of blue coveralls, and carried what looked like a toolbox in his hand.

"Who are you? What the hell do you mean—"

"My name is Carter, Mr. St. James, and we're going to talk."

Carter went near, measured, drew a deep breath, and

struck. It was a clean jolt, with all his weight behind it, straight to the chin. Hannibal St. James went down and out and lay breathing stentoriously on his thick-piled carpet.

First thing, Carter pulled the pants off the resting man. Underneath he was wearing shorts, which Carter also tugged off. When you're naked you lose your dignity, and loss of dignity loosens the tongue. Carter had other arrows in his quiver and he intended to use them all.

He dragged St. James to a massive armchair and set him into it. Then he used the friction tape from the toolbox to tie him into it. Then he tested. He had him good. Hannibal St. James was firmly affixed. He was as much a part of the armchair as the upholstery.

Carter opened a bottle of Chivas Regal. He put ice and water into a pitcher. He took the bottle, the pitcher, and a glass to an end table beside a chair facing the immobilized man. He lit a cigarette, sat, drank, smoked, and waited. Finally St. James opened his eyes.

"Well, hello there," Carter said cheerfully.

"You bastard, what do you want?"

"Your cooperation, Mr. St. James. Or your ass."

"Go to hell."

"Assuredly I will one day," Carter offered, "but in the meantime I might send you ahead of me."

"Do you know who you are dealing with?"

"I sure do," Carter replied, opening his toolbox and spreading papers in front of the other man. "The biggest fish I've ever hung out to dry."

"I'll hang the American government out to dry for this!"

"Ah," Carter said, "I see you are quite aware that I am a government agent."

St. James clamped his jaw shut and glared.

"Your hired killer is in the Old Bailey right now, St.

James. Here is his signed confession, four pages. I think you'll notice that he names you, quite specifically."

Carter slowly flipped the pages, making sure that St. James read every word and took in the perfectly forged signature.

"And here is the signed confession of one Rosario Duncan. It doesn't implicate you, of course, but it does state that he has worked for Layman in the past, on illegal deals of which you or one of your companies was the prime beneficiary."

"They are lying. The word of two criminals against my word?"

Carter shrugged. "Here is an indictment that will be filed against you and your companies at nine tomorrow morning by the International Maritime Commission, for the instigation of piracy on the high seas. And *this* indictment is by Lloyd's of London, for attempted fraud. It, too, will be filed tomorrow morning."

St. James, cool-eyed but sweating, laughed. "They can stand in line. I've had thirty indictments filed against me in as many years. None of them ever stuck."

"True," Carter said, "but when they are filed in conjunction with the *Thor I*'s sinking, your stock on the London and New York exchanges will plummet. That, along with your losses and Lloyd's tying you in knots for years, will practically bankrupt you."

A full minute passed. "What do you want?"

"The entire setup with El Adwan and what he plans to do with the *Thor I*."

Time passed. A lot of time passed.

Carter could sense that Hannibal St. James was beginning to fly distress signals. He was sweating, twitching, involuntarily nodding. His lips were dry and he was swallowing a lot of air.

Carter smoked and sipped his drink.

When the answer came, the Killmaster was surprised. He actually thought that he had nailed the old thief.

"Carter, or whoever you are, I don't have the slightest idea what you're talking about. I have never heard of this El Adwan. Mr. Horst Layman was fired from my employ a week ago. My accountants will substantiate that. As for this Duncan you speak of . . . I've never heard of him."

Carter got tense but held his ground. "And Oliver Estes?"

"A good man, but flawed," St. James replied. "Also fired from my employ. I have proof that for years he has been embezzling from my companies."

The guy was no wimp, Carter thought as he mashed out his cigarette and finished his drink.

"Mr. St. James, you're a hard and clever man."

From the small of his back, Carter took a short-barreled .22 revolver. Methodically, he removed shells from his jacket pocket and slipped them into the gun.

"What the hell do you think you're doing?"

"It's small, only a twenty-two, but the shells are hollow-point. One of them going in your left ear will do about the same damage as a forty-five."

"You're crazy!" St. James said, laughing but without any humor. "Even if you do it, you won't get ten feet. There are forty people out by that pool!"

"That there are, Mr. St. James, but the doors are closed and the music by the pool is loud and a twenty-two caliber revolver doesn't make much of a bang."

Silence. The squat, heavy body strained against the tape. The veins of the neck bulged, jaw muscles clamped to tight knots. The eyes were filmy.

Carter flipped the cylinder closed.

"We'll leak everything to the papers tonight. Naturally, reporters will be calling you. You will realize that your plan has failed. You won't be able to stand the disgrace . . ."

"What? Me? Kill myself? Nobody would believe it!"

"Oh, I think they will," Carter said, taking an official-looking document from his pocket and crossing to the desk.

"What is that?"

Carter floated it in the air for a second and dropped it in the top drawer. "It's your permit for this gun, dated six months ago. It's very official, Mr. St. James, I assure you. The master copy is on file at Scotland Yard."

"Good Lord, man, this is cold-blooded murder!"

"That it is, Mr. St. James, that it is." Carter moved toward him, idly holding the revolver in his right hand.

St. James squirmed and lurched against the tape that bound him. The sweat ran in rivers on his face and body. Carter could smell him.

"What the hell kind of a man are you?" he said, his voice almost a squeak.

"A bad man, Hannibal, a very bad man."

Carter freed his left hand. St. James tried to swing on him, but before the blow landed, Carter had shoved his thumb, hard, into the soft part at the front of his shoulder just below the collarbone. The left arm immediately went limp.

"What the . . . ?"

"Frozen, Hannibal. I bruised the nerve. Your arm will be that way, useless, for about three minutes. There's another nerve in your hand, right here between the thumb and first finger . . . does the same thing."

Carter squeezed there, and the fingers that had been fluttering immediately went limp. The Killmaster then placed the gun in St. James's hand and wound the fingers carefully around it. He brought hand and gun up before St. James's eyes. Carefully, he pulled the hammer back until it clicked.

"You still think it won't look like suicide, Hannibal? See, I even know you're left-handed."

The man's chin sank down as his eyes closed. There was froth on his lips.

Carter brought the hand and gun up. He ground the barrel into St. James's left ear.

"Good-bye, Hannibal."

"All right . . . all right, dammit, I'll tell you what I know!"

Carter removed the gun from his ear and St. James leaned forward and vomited.

"They're probably on board by now."

"How?" Carter said.

St. James was still shaking like a leaf and now he really stank. "For God's sake, man, untie me and let me clean up!"

"*How?*"

"In the foodstuff containers. They're stored in the aft hold near the galley. They went into them last night after they were loaded in the warehouse."

"How many are there?"

"Thirteen, plus El Adwan himself."

"All fourteen in the containers?"

Silence. Carter clicked the hammer on the revolver.

"No. One was planted before the ship left Japan. He's the third assistant cook."

"What's his job in the operation?"

"Food poisoning, the evening meal."

"That means they hit tonight."

"Yes, around midnight."

"And what's the sailing time?"

"Five in the morning."

Carter thought for a moment. They were probably out of the containers already and spread through the bowels of the giant ship. There was even a good chance that in the vastness of the supertanker they had already started to plant explosives.

"What's the plan once they've taken the ship?"

"They sail through the Strait of Hormuz, around Oman, and into the Indian Ocean."

"You're doing good, Hannibal. Keep doing good."

"Once they clear the Gulf of Oman, they break radio silence . . . make their demands."

"And those are?"

"Fifty million American dollars, dropped by helicopter."

"And then?"

"They set the charges and then transfer to a freighter. When the freighter is safely in Aden, they radio back the combination to the master circuit to cut off the detonators."

Carter leaned forward and put the gun in St. James's crotch. "That's the plan for Lloyd's benefit. Now, what *really* happens, St. James? I know you don't want that ship inspected. It has to be sunk."

The man's jaw was shaking so much he could hardly speak.

"It . . . it was a trade-off. El Adwan is going to sink it in the Strait of Hormuz, crosswise in the channel."

"Jesus," Carter growled.

The Strait of Hormuz is the only access to the land-locked Persian Gulf. Block it with something the size of the *Thor I* and it would be years before the Gulf was usuable again.

"Let me fill in the blanks," Carter growled. "You recoup the loss of the *Thor I* from Lloyd's, scrap the *Thor II*, and because of the instant oil shortage caused by the cutoff of the Persian Gulf, your Octagon reserves around the world double in price. Right?"

Carter had risen and moved around behind the man. As he spoke, he had withdrawn a hypodermic ampule from the toolbox.

"Well, Hannibal, that's about the way it's supposed to go, isn't it?"

"Yes . . . yes," the man gasped.

"What about the hundred and eighty-odd crewmen? Any provision for them?"

Silence.

"And the oil? A sea of crude oil in the Indian Ocean. Evidently you didn't give a shit about that, did you, Hannibal?"

Silence.

"Who's their lookout in Kuwait, Hannibal? They have to have someone making sure they aren't nailed before they get the *Thor* moving. Who is it?"

Silence.

"Who is it!"

"It . . . it's my chief dispatcher. He has an office in the harbor tower."

"Thanks, Hannibal. Have a nice sleep, you son of a bitch."

Carter stuck the hypodermic into his neck.

FIFTEEN

"Nick, this is Colonel Vernon MacCreedy."

Carter shook hands with a man that had him by three inches in height. He had straw-blond hair and a cheerful face with dancing blue eyes. He looked like a young lawyer, a businessman, or someone who should be staring out of a television set with a beautiful woman on each arm.

As the Killmaster had observed so often in his long and rather eventful career, looks could indeed be deceiving.

A year before, MacCreedy had walked up a flight of tenement steps in Northern Ireland with only a handgun and a shattered left shoulder to take out four terrorist gunmen.

"Your men on board, Colonel?"

"An even dozen, sir, combat ready and with all the gear you asked for."

"They're all volunteers, Colonel?" Carter asked.

MacCreedy smiled. "The whole SAS is volunteers, sir."

Carter turned to Jonathan Hart-Davis. "How are we set up?"

"Full cooperation of the Kuwaitis. They look the other way, we do our own laundry."

"Landing clearance?"

Hart-Davis nodded. "We've got it all the way. Here comes your final passenger."

Carter turned just as a four-door Rover pulled up beside them. The woman inside didn't wait for the driver to come around and open the door for her. She opened the door herself and crawled out.

Carter really hadn't imagined Carolyn Reed, but even if he had he wouldn't have imagined this. She was tall, quite beautiful, and quite angry.

"Miss Reed, thank you for coming. I'm Jonathan Hart-Davis."

She swung her briefcase to her left hand and shook hands with her right. "It's about time someone paid some attention to my report."

"Er . . . ah, yes. This is Nick Carter. He'll be in charge of the operation."

"You're the American."

"That's right."

"I won't hold it against you."

"Thank you," Carter said. "Shall we board?"

She led the way to the gaping open hatch of the big cargo jet.

• • •

When they were leveled off, MacCreedy huddled his men around Carter and Carolyn Reed. The woman opened her briefcase and passed a blue-jacketed folder to each of the men.

"These are detailed, deck-by-deck plans of every inch of the *Thor I*." When this was done, she turned to Carter. "All right, what do you need to know?"

"One hundred and eighty-some men. Where would the terrorists put them to keep them out of their hair? With a ship as big as the *Thor*, there has to be one or more blind spots from the decks or superstructure. Where are they? In case of high-powered automatic fire, what can't we hit? Where are the stress points in the holds that explosives would do the worst and quickest damage? That'll do for a start."

Carolyn Reed let a tiny smile curl the corners of her lips, took a deep breath, and started to teach.

Alfredo Dinebar slipped through the opening in the deck of the number two engine room and slid down the rungs of the ladder.

He had just finished his watch, but he wouldn't be heading for the galley and evening chow just yet. Alfredo wanted a smoke, and the kind of cigarettes he smoked didn't go over too well with some of his fellow crewmen.

Lighting up and dragging the acrid smoke deep into his lungs, he moved aft along the five-foot-wide walkway between the inner hall and the huge aft storage tank.

"Ah, man, lotsa crude. If I had just some of that crude, I'd never have to ship out on one of these stinkin' wagons again."

Dinebar dropped down to the lower "B" level and

turned into the valveway between the two aft tanks. Just as he made the turn, he slid to a stop.

One of the big walkway templates had been lifted on end, and over the hole two men were feeding wire down to a third.

Jesus, Dinebar thought, *a damned repair division crew and I walk right into them!*

Quickly, he mashed out his cigarette and fanned the air around his head. He was about to step back around the corner, when he was spotted.

"Say, man," Dinebar said with a laugh, "we ain't even out of first port and the damn thing's fallin' apart already. How about that, man?"

The repairman was three feet from Alfredo when his hand came up holding a silenced 9mm Beretta.

He shot Alfredo Dinebar directly between the eyes.

The light rap on the door awakened Captain Alonso Wakefield immediately. He came up to a sitting position on his bunk and snapped on the light.

The brand-new Rolex his wife had given him for his new command said eleven o'clock.

"Yes, yes, come in," he called.

"Sorry to disturb you, Captain, but we've got a problem."

"The umbilical cord?"

"No, sir, the pumping is going fine. We have a tank and a half full, fore and aft. They will soon be switching to the last two tanks."

"Well, what is it, Mr. Richardson?"

"It's the mid-watch, sir. Over half of them have reported to sick bay with stomach cramps."

"Half the watch?"

"Yes, sir."

"All right. Get volunteers for overtime off the eve-watch, and have the cook send sandwiches up. Any idea what the hell it is?"

"No, sir. But I've told the infirmary to let us know whenever they find out."

"All right, Mr. Richardson. I'll be up. Can't sleep worth a damn anyway."

The first officer backed out, and Captain Wakefield started to pull on his pants.

Damn, he thought, *haven't even taken on payload yet and the malingering has already started!*

Carter looked around at the grim faces in the semicircle, nodded his satisfaction, and turned back to Carolyn Reed.

"Good job. That's the most comprehensive crash course on supertankers I've ever heard."

"Thank you," she replied, and turned to the men herself. "Any further questions?"

"Yeah," said a fresh-faced young sergeant. "What's yer favorite pub in London?"

Carolyn smiled. "Why do you ask?"

"Obvious, ain't it? I want to run into ya!"

She laughed. "Tell you what. All of you come through this without a scratch and I'll throw the party."

"Attention, attention," the intercom blared. "We're one hour from set down. I have received word that your ground transportation is ready and waiting."

Colonel MacCreedy turned to Carter. "I've already got an idea or two."

"Me, too." Carter nodded. "Let's hash it over."

"Do you need me?" Carolyn asked.

"It would help," Carter replied.

"Then you've got me."

She stood and with the two men moved forward to the lighted chart table just aft of the cockpit.

"Bridge, this is Dobbin."

"Yes, Chief, this is the Captain."

"Captain, I'm getting a strange reading in the loaded tanks."

"How so?"

"I'm showing more intake than capacity. And, also, the sway ratio is off. The damn stuff is splashing around in there like beer in a barrel."

"Are your tanks balanced, Chief?"

"Aye, sir."

"Then recalibrate the gauges and give me another reading."

"Aye, sir."

"Captain . . ."

"Yes, Mr. Richardson?"

"It's food poisoning, sir."

"Oh, Christ. How bad?"

"Minor serious, sir. But it's hit some of the day watch now."

"How many able men do we have?"

"Thirty-three crew."

"Any officers?"

"No, sir. Evidently it didn't hit the wardroom galley."

"All right. Get volunteers for overtime, and log it."

"Aye, sir."

"Abu?"

"Yes."

"All of our people are in place. Less than a third of the crew are on deck."

"The time?"

"Eleven-forty."

"We move now."

The big jet had scarcely rocked to a halt when men poured from the dropped hatch. In minutes the equipment was unloaded and reloaded on two personnel carriers.

Behind the personnel carriers, a gray Mercedes sedan was parked with a uniformed officer in the driver's seat.

"Nick Carter."

"Major Assad Dalfi, Mr. Carter. Here is the information you requested."

Carter snatched the sheet from the man. "Clark Magam, born Yorkshire, 1950 . . . fluent Arabic . . . thanks." He ran to the rear of the first personnel carrier. "Colonel . . ."

"Yes, sir?"

"I know you have six men fluent in Arabic. Do any of them speak English with a Yorkshire accent?"

"I do, sir. Name's Lamb."

"Come with me, Lamb. Colonel, I'll meet you."

Carter, with First Sergeant Arnold Lamb at his heels, ran back to the Mercedes.

"Let's go, Major. You know where."

"Yes, sir!"

Clark Magam lowered high-powered field glasses and rubbed his eyes. It was five minutes until midnight. They would be close now, probably on the move.

He leaned over to a pipe rack, took a pipe, filled it, tamped it, lit it, and produced evil-smelling fumes. He was a little man with a seamed face, a nearly bald head, and a sepulchral voice. He was nearsighted and wore heavy-rimmed glassed, thick-lenses glasses behind which his eyes swam like fish in a bowl.

But he could see well enough for this night's work. And this night's work would give him more money than he ever dreamed of.

He had always told himself that doing whatever the old man asked—and asking no questions about it—would pay off. Two days from now he would be out of this hateful place and back in England.

He was about to raise the binoculars back to his eyes, when the locked door behind him burst from its hinges. He got only halfway turned before his eyeglasses were knocked from his face and a fist flattened his navel against his backbone.

"Get his glasses!"

Magam's glasses were reinstated and he saw a gun nearly a mile long being waved in front of his eyes. Behind the gun was a grinning face and the meanest pair of eyes Magam's had ever seen.

"Know what this is? It's a nine-millimeter Luger with a silencer. It comes with hollow-tipped slugs dipped in cyanide. Anywhere I shoot you, you die. Do you want to die?"

"No . . . no!"

"Good, Mr. Magam from Yorkshire, because I don't want you to die. But if you don't answer all my questions as fast as I ask them, I'm going to shove this silencer down your throat and blow the back of your head all over that window."

Mr. Clark Magam couldn't answer fast enough.

"Captain, Dobbins here . . ."

"Yes, Chief?"

"Sir, I don't know what the hell . . . sir, my hatch . . ."

Suddenly there was a burst of automatic rifle fire on

the intercom and the garbled scream of a dying man. The scream was still echoing off the three officers on the bridge when there was an explosion. The locked hatch to the bridge exploded from its bolts and the whole area was filled with acrid smoke.

First Officer Richardson was farther from the hatch than the others. When he saw the two men—machine pistols at the ready—emerge through the smoke, he dived for the weapons on the nearby bulkhead.

He barely got the case open when a burst from one of the machine pistols shattered his chest. He was thrown over the main bank of computers and slammed to the deck, dead.

The man who had fired—tall and rangy, with long black hair and a heavy, flowing beard—jammed the barrel of his pistol into the belly of the *Thor I*'s stunned skipper.

"Captain Wakefield, my name is Abu El Adwan. I am in the process of relieving you of your command."

"The bloody hell . . ."

The blow from the steel butt of the machine pistol came so swiftly that Wakefield didn't even see the movement. It struck him in the shoulder, driving him back, and before he could regain his balance the barrel sliced a deep, three-inch gash in his cheek.

"You will do as I say, Captain Wakefield, or every man under your command will be shot. Do you understand?"

Silence.

The two men stood glaring at one another, neither blinking.

"Do you understand!"

"I will not give up my ship to bloody terrorists."

El Adwan turned to the other officer. He flipped the

machine pistol to single shot and killed the officer at point-blank range.

"Do you understand, Captain Wakefield?"

The captain swallowed, blinked his eyes once, and then averted them from the young officer's corpse. "I understand."

El Adwan found the proper switches on the ship's inner communication console, and began using them.

"Radio room?"

"This is Antonia, Abu. The radio room is secure."

"Familiarize yourself with the equipment. I'll be right back to you."

One by one, El Adwan went through the ship's stations, and one by one he found them secure.

"Abu, this is Jadak at the main power plant."

"Yes, Jadak?"

"Five hands on duty. We have three. The two others are in the heating and air-conditioning plant and refuse to budge."

"Are you in communication?"

"We are."

"Then give the two of them one minute to surrender. If they don't, inform them that you will shoot their mates one by one until they do."

"Right away."

"My God," Wakefield gasped, "you're a barbarian!"

"Not at all, Captain. I am a businessman, and, at times, a patriot. Now, shut up."

El Adwan made some calculations on a pad of paper. He checked them twice, and then turned again to Wakefield.

"By my tally, I am missing eleven men. You will call on all stations for any man hiding on the ship to surrender himself to my people. They will have five minutes. If all hands are not accounted for by that time, I will begin executing men in the forward crew quarters."

The captain knew he had no choice. He stepped to the console and flipped the all-stations switch.

"All hands, attention all hands. This is Captain Wakefield. We have been taken over by terrorists. They are in control of the ship. It is futile, lads. Give yourselves up and save your mates."

"Excellent, Captain. Pour yourself a cup of tea. In fact, pour two."

In ten minutes, El Adwan ran through the stations again. All hands were accounted for.

"Antonia?"

"Here."

"Contact Jellyfish!"

Carter's eyes burned as he stared through the night glasses at the bulk of the *Thor I*. All the floods and above-deck lights were on. The only movement was on the tugs as the fitters constantly checked the flow and the huge clamp that held the pumping tube to the side feed of the ship.

"If they're moving, they sure as hell aren't showing themselves," he growled.

Beside him, SAS Sergeant Lamb merely grunted in reply, adjusted his volume and frequency controls, and, now and then, glanced over at the trussed-up figure of Clark Magam.

"It's a quarter past twelve. Unless they met resistance, they should have touched base by now." Carter moved to Magam as he spoke. "You see that commando knife on the sergeant's belt?"

"Yes . . ."

Magram was petrified. Carter was surprised he hadn't already peed his pants.

"Let me tell you, Magam, that the sergeant can peel three quarters of the skin from your body before you'll die."

"For God's sake, man, what do you want?" Magam cried. "I've told you everything!"

"Have you, Magam?" Carter hissed. "Have you given us the right frequencies?"

"I swear . . ."

Suddenly the two three-inch speakers above the console crackled to life.

"Got something, sir . . ."

Carter moved quickly back to Lamb's side as a woman's voice came through the speakers.

"Jellyfish, this is Shark. Shark calling Jellyfish. Come in!"

"This is Jellyfish, Shark. Over."

"I read you nine and fine, Jellyfish. Over."

"You are four and floating, Shark. Can you ease up with a test?"

"Going up . . . test . . . test . . . test . . ."

"There, Shark, lock in. You are eight and steady. Over."

There was silence for a few seconds, and then a man's voice, speaking guttural Arabic, came on.

"What is the first star in the desert night?"

"The one that shines the brightest," Lamb replied in barely accented Arabic, and Carter squeezed his shoulder.

The woman's voice returned. "We are secure, Jellyfish. What is your scope? Over."

"Port side, bow, to about one hundred yards short of

stern. Around bow on starboard side almost amidships. Over."

"Thank you, Jellyfish. We will adjust. Fifteen-minute checks unless you spot something. Clear? Over."

"Clear, Shark. Out."

The two men sighed in tandem relief.

"They bought it," Carter said, and returned the glasses to his eyes.

Less than a minute later, he saw men floating out onto the upper decks. No firearms were showing, but that meant nothing. Each of them moved to man a lookout spot beyond Lamb's range of vision.

All of them were in place when the remainder of the starboard spotlights came on, flooding the sea with light for nearly a hundred yards.

"Time to go," Carter said. "You've got the picture?"

"Yes, sir. One-ten sharp, I spot surface movement off the starboard bow."

"Good man."

Carter raced to the door and down the stairs to the waiting Mercedes.

SIXTEEN

Each and every one of the SAS men was a highly trained machine. When they moved, they did it with stealth and grace. Hardly a sound was made and there was no wasted movement.

Fifteen minutes before the planned diversion, four men equipped with finger-gripped suction cups went up the seven-story-high hull of the *Thor I*. Twenty yards apart on the starboard side, thirty yards aft the hull, they looked like tiny gray crabs moving through a field of rust.

They covered the height in exactly two minutes and seven seconds. Another five seconds to clamp three blocks of stronger, clamp-held devices, and four ropes spiraled down the side of the ship. The ropes were knotted every thirty inches so the men climbing always had a handhold, and were stabilized by the insteps of both feet on a knot.

Two minutes before Jellyfish would alert Shark to surface movement off the stern to starboard, all thirteen men hung, swaying gently, seven stories above the sea.

"Shark, this is Jellyfish. Come in!"

"Go ahead, Jellyfish."

"I have surface movement about two hundred yards off your stern, starboard side. Over."

"Can you identify? Over."

"Negative, Shark. It would help if you could lift a couple of the starboard floods."

"Will do, Jellyfish. Keep me informed. Out." Antonia Perini shook the blond hair from her eyes and flipped the console switch marked Bridge.

"Abu . . ."

"Here."

"Jellyfish has a sighting about two hundred yards off the stern, starboard side."

"A boat?"

"Surface movement. He wants you to lift one or two of the starboard floods."

"I'll take care of it."

El Adwan lifted the walkie from his belt and instructed the five lookouts. Instantly, two of them were scampering up the ladders on the starboard side of the superstructure toward the floods. The other three hit the rail themselves, night glasses to their eyes.

At MacCreedy's hand signal, the top four men rolled over the bow lip and hoisted themselves to the main deck. They had barely flattened out—almost invisible in their hooded gray wet suits against the matching deck—when four more men followed.

Once again there was no wasted time or movement. The first four men moved thirty yards to the two massive screens guarding the air intake for the air-conditioning plant far below in the bowels of the ship. By the time the last man had scrambled over the bow, the screens were off and the first four were already descending.

Again, like crabs, using the sneakers on their feet and the fins—worn over their sneakers while swimming—on their hands, they made their way down the slick steel sides of the vents, seven to a side.

Neither of the enormous fans were turning. In fact they were hardly ever operational in port. Smaller fans, generator-powered, saved fuel when the ship wasn't moving.

When the screens were off, each of the men slithered between the blades into the lower vent area. This was level, and twenty feet into it was the repair trap. Once through this, they crawled along a narrow catwalk above the huge unit itself. A hatch at the end of the catwalk opened into the engineer's ready room.

It was empty.

Two by two, they emerged from the catwalk hatchways and padded silently to the hatch leading into the forward power plant. MacCreedy cautiously rose until he could peer through the window.

It had been three minutes and forty-one seconds since the first four men had come over the bow.

"Jellyfish, this is Shark. We have spotted nothing."

"The light helps, Shark. I can't see it now either. Guess I'm just jumpy. Over."

"Better to be safe, Jellyfish. Stay with me. Out."

Sergeant Lamb lifted the glasses and sighed with relief. They were all up, over, and out of sight before the five men drifted back to their assigned places.

MacCreedy turned to Carter. He held up one hand and curled all five fingers.

Five prisoners.

He held up one finger on his other hand.

One guard.

Carter nodded and slipped in beside him, the silenced and compact Sten Model IV up and ready.

MacCreedy spun the revolving lock on the watertight hatch. It moved silently. When it stopped, the colonel turned to Carter.

The Killmaster nodded.

The hatch was yanked open.

Carter fired a three-shot burst from four feet, tearing the side of the man's head off as he was turning.

In four seconds, all the SAS men were in the forward engine ready room and Carter was interrogating the chief engineer.

No, there had been no call down from the bridge since the initial takeover. Yes, the five of them had been left below to monitor the pressure gauges and keep checking the automatic oilers.

As Carter asked questions and got answers, the two men who would be part of his unit moved in behind him. There would be three units, with Carter's designated Unit One. Unit Two—with five men commanded by Colonel MacCreedy—would move forward to free the crew. Unit Three—under Major Culham—would search for and dismantle the explosives.

Units Two and Three had already moved out when Carter gave his last instructions to the chief engineer.

"If any of them show up down here, use his gun and don't be sad about it."

"It'll be a pleasure, sir."

Carter, followed by his two men, moved up to "A" lower level and aft.

Fourteen terrorists all told, with one dead and five as lookouts on the main deck. Carter guessed that El Adwan would be on the bridge with at least one other man.

That left six they would have to find.

The Killmaster hoped against hope that the scenario that Carolyn Reed had set up for them was at least eighty percent accurate.

"Saed, this is Abu. How is it?"

"Steady. They are on the last two tanks . . . approaching half."

"What do you estimate?"

"A little over an hour."

"Excellent," El Adwan replied. "Let me know the moment they top off."

Ten feet from the blown hatch of the tank control room, Carter heard the man's voice and halted.

Using sign language, he gestured one of his men forward. The SAS man dropped to his belly and, like a snake, slithered forward until he was flat on the floor adjacent to the hatch.

One quick look and he held up one finger. Carter gave him a thumbs-up sign, and backed down the passageway with his second man moving in step.

They went up another deck and then aft again until they were directly below the forward section of the superstructure. Carter dropped to a hunkering position and took the walkie-talkie from his belt. Livingstone, the remaining man with him, checked the passageway to the next turn and nodded back.

Carter depressed the red alert button once and waited. A two count later, the red light on his own walkie blinked twice. Another two count and it blinked three times. Colonel MacCreedy and Major Culham were in areas where they could talk.

"Carter here. 'A' upper-level deck. Ready to go up. Valve control is covered. One man. Colonel?"

"Two of them in the forward crew quarters. Covered. I am at the aft crew quarters now. Two here, as well. Over."

"Major?"

"So far, Miss Reed has been right on the nose. We have hit six jackpots, all exactly at the hull stress points where she guessed they would be. Over."

"Are they neutralized?" Carter said.

"Yes . . . wait a second . . ." It was more like ten. "Sir?"

"Go ahead," Carter said.

"We just found the first one on the tanks. Sir, it's remote-controlled like the ones on the hull, but it's locked into a relay. If we crack it, sir, it will automatically pulse. Over."

"That means it can't be cracked? Over."

"Maybe, sir, but it's going to be tricky. We'll have to dismantle in the exact sequence or we'll all go boom, sir. Over."

"Okay, Major, stay with it. Out."

Carter made a mental note. If the radio was manned by a woman, and she was alone, and there was one with El Adwan on the bridge, they had all fourteen accounted for.

"Jadak . . . Jadak, Abu here! Can you hear me?"

For the third time, the inner-ship line from the engine room came alive, but only with buzzing and crackling. If there was voice in there, El Adwan couldn't hear it.

"Dammit, Jadak . . ."

"We have been having trouble with that line since we left Japan," the captain lied, his knowledge telling him that, with the ship's sealed communications units, that kind of steady interference could never occur.

El Adwan turned to the dark-haired woman at the door. "Pilon, go down to the forward engine room and check, just in case."

"As you wish, Abu," she replied, and left.

"Antonia?"

"Yes, Abu."

"Anything more from Jellyfish?"

"Nothing beyond the last regular check."

El Adwan checked with the rest of his people and found them all in place and everything quiet.

He was just turning from the console when Captain Wakefield lunged at him. It was an unskilled and stupid charge, considering the bigger man's swiftness and dexterity.

El Adwan countered the blow easily and slammed the butt of his machine pistol viciously against the point of the older man's jaw. Wakefield dropped like a stone to the deck, and the terrorist leader kicked him viciously in the side.

"Stupid old man!"

The communications center was one deck below the bridge and just forward of it. Carter was halfway up the last ladder to that deck, with Livingstone right behind him, when he heard the sound of footsteps approaching on the steel deck of the passageway above.

Both men slid back down using the handrail, and darted through the nearest hatch, closing it behind them. It was the chart room, and through an open hatch Carter could see radar equipment. Leaving the other man to guard the hatch, the Killmaster did a quick recon. Finding both areas empty, he returned.

"Sir, it's a woman," Livingstone whispered, nodding toward the passageway.

Cautiously Carter eased his head up until he could peer through the double glass. A short stocky woman wearing fatigues, a handgun holstered at her hip, and with an AK-47 slung over her shoulder, was walking forward to the next ladder.

"Well, now," Carter murmured as she disappeared, "I wonder if that's our radio operator."

Major Bryan Culham peered over the shoulders of the two crouched men with sweat pouring off his forehead into his eyes. He took a deep breath, and then sighed as the plastic case came apart and there was no mishap.

"Six wires," one of the men said, "just like the other four."

"Are they in the same sequence?"

"Yeah, but nothing tells me which wire is the relay."

"Damn," Culham said. "Let's try the last one."

At the top of the ladder leading down to the forward ready room that controlled one of the two massive diesels, the brunette called Pilon paused.

"Jadak? . . . Jadak, are you there? Is everything all right?"

There was no answer.

Pilon unlimbered the automatic rifle from her shoulder and moved down the ladder, step by step. At the bottom,

she went to her knees and dived, belly-up, through the
hatch. The moment she hit the deck she covered the room
with the muzzle of the weapon.

Nothing. Empty. No sign.

And then she saw it, a dark stain on the green deck
padding. Cautiously, she touched it with a finger and
tasted.

Blood.

Alert now, using only seconds, the woman moved in
a wide arc around the stain until she found a drop of
blood, and then another, until it became a trail. It led
her toward the starboard walkway and then down, toward
the lower decks and aft.

Colonel MacCreedy left his final two officers to cover
the two terrorists, and went forward again. Amidships,
he went down to the lowest deck level and checked his
position.

He was two hatches away from the generator room.

Pilon paused to orient herself. She was on the lowest
level of the ship now, just about amidships, and moving
forward.

The trail of blood had petered out twice, but by trial
and error she had picked it up both times. The last spot
was a foot in front of the hatch that led into the generator
room.

She crouched and cautiously moved forward. The spin
lock wouldn't rotate. The hatch was locked from the
inside.

What would Abu want her to do? Was the blood
Jadak's? Or had he killed or wounded part of the crew
and this is where they fled, with Jadak pursuing them?

The decision was made for her when she peered through

the double-thick windows. They were masked. That could mean only one thing.

She set aside her gun and took two blocks of plastique from her utility belt. Quickly, she molded the puttylike explosive into the cracks around the hatch, liberally at the lock and two hinges. A mercury detonator with a ten-second fuse was inserted into the mass, and then she pushed the small button on the call box beside the hatch. Faintly, she could hear the attention buzzer inside through the hatch.

She put her lips close to the call box. "I know you are in there. I don't know what you have done with my comrade, but I am giving you ten seconds to open this hatch or I will blow it open. Do you hear me?"

Three seconds passed and then a voice, in Cockney English, replied. "We've got yer man in here and we've got his gun. If ya blow the door, I'll kill him."

"Let me speak to him."

Pause. "No."

Pilon smiled. "I think Jadak is already dead. I'll give you to the count of three. One . . ."

"Don't move, don't even twitch, or I'll cut you exactly in half."

Pilon's whole being, her mind-set, was made up of instincts. Instantly, she rolled to the side, grasped her gun, and kept rolling. Out of the corner of her eye she saw the figure in the gray wet suit.

She came up on one knee, but her right hand wasn't fast enough.

All six slugs from the Sten's double three-shot burst stitched her body from pelvis to breast. She died before her body hit the bulkhead.

The gray wet suit moved to the hatch and gently removed the mercury detonator from the plastique. He then tugged the woman's bloody body away from the bulkhead so it could be seen from inside the generator room.

This done, he leaned toward the talk box himself. "This is SAS Colonel Vernon MacCreedy. I need to get in there. Take the mask off the window and take a look."

Carter and Livingstone had just hit the passageway about thirty feet from the open hatch to the radio room, when their question was answered.

"Shark, this is Jellyfish."

"Go ahead, Jellyfish."

"Fifteen-minute check. Nil, all's calm and quiet. Over."

"Check, Jellyfish. I'm told topping off is about ten minutes. We should be making way in an hour. Out."

Carter and Livingstone traded satisfied looks. Obviously there were two women. And the one they had spotted coming down had been descending from the bridge. The short brunette had been the "man" with El Adwan.

And then they got another break. Antonia Perini spoke again.

"Bridge, are you there, Abu?"

"Yes. The fool of a captain tried to take me."

"Oh, God," said the woman. "Did you have to kill him?"

A laugh. "No, but he'll be sailing us toward the strait with a broken jaw. Anything from Jellyfish?"

"All clear."

"Check."

Now they knew that Abu El Adwan was indeed on the bridge.

Carter motioned Livingstone forward until he was positioned outside the radio room, just as the other SAS officer was positioned outside the valve control room.

Then Carter slithered back forward and moved around the enormous superstructure until he was at the ladder leading up to the bridge.

The red light on his walkie-talkie was blinking.

"Carter here," he whispered.

"MacCreedy. I've killed one of them, a woman."

"Short, built wide, dark hair?" Carter asked.

"You've got it. I'm in the generator room. I'm leaving my walkie with the chief engineer, name's Harris. You can give him the word on cutoff."

"And?" Carter said.

"We have two AKs. I'm taking two of the crew with me topside. We can cover the five lookouts."

"Good thinking," Carter said. "That makes it complete."

Yeah, he added to himself, *complete if Major Culham and Unit Three don't blow us to hell!*

He lifted the walkie-talkie back to his lips.

"Jadak . . . Pilon . . . dammit, somebody down there answer me!"

El Adwan slammed his palm against the console and cursed again.

His senses, tuned over years of living on the edge, were telling him something was not right. First Jadak, and now Pilon.

What the hell was going on?

"Kroll . . . Kroll, where are you?"

"I am on the fantail, main deck. What is it?"

"Get down to the forward engine room. Jadak and Pilon should be down there, but I can't get an answer out of them."

"What's wrong?"

"Dammit, if I knew I wouldn't be sending you down there. Move!"

El Adwan slumped into the captain's swing chair, and for the tenth time checked the loads in his AK-47 and pistol.

Then he fingered the battery-powered pulse-sender on his belt, the unit that, with one twist of a dial and one push of a button, would send them all to hell.

"Major . . . Carter here."

"Yes, sir," Culham said, making a conscious effort to keep his voice level.

"How is it?"

"The search is complete, sir. Six jackpots on the hull, all neutralized. We have found eight more on the tanks. We are opening the last one now."

"And . . .?"

"Nothing to report further until we get it open, sir."

"Are you sure you've got them all?"

"Yes, sir. We've done two complete sweeps and that's it, unless they've placed some above decks. And, according to the Reed woman, that would be highly unlikely."

"And you agree?"

"I do, sir."

"All right," Carter said. "We've got two dead and all the rest are covered. Our main honcho is on the bridge, alone. I'm going up now."

"Good luck, sir."

"Good luck to you, Major. And for God's sake, if you find the relay key, let me know right away."

"Will do, sir."

Major Culham returned the walkie to his belt and again dropped to his knees beside the two men working over the small plastic box.

"Anything?"

"Maybe, just maybe," one of them replied. "See the fresh solder on the blue and white wires?"

"I see it."

"It's the same on the rest of them. They've changed the order from the way the wires were originally set up."

Culham ran a finger along his forehead and flicked away the sweat. "That probably means either the blue or the white is the relay."

"Yes, sir, it does."

"Question is, which one?"

"Yes, sir, that sure as hell is the question."

Carter heaved himself up over the top of the last overhang and crawled forward through the maze of radio antennae and radar scoops until he was just at the edge.

From here he had a clear view directly down into the bridge.

The forward, port, and starboard sides of the main bridge were all glass. He could see Captain Wakefield sitting in a swivel chair holding his head in his hands.

The only other occupant was Abu El Adwan . . . tall, bearded, long black hair—obviously a wig—to his shoulders.

Carter sighted the Sten.

There was only a fifty-fifty chance that a burst would get him before he could hit the pulser at his belt. The thick glass would deflect the slugs.

One large pane of the window was open. Each time El Adwan spoke into the control console, Carter could hear every word.

Now, if the man would only walk in front of the open window. . . .

•   •   •

"Abu?"

"Yes."

"We're topped. The tugs are leaving now."

"Good," El Adwan replied. "We'll get under way at once. Kroll, where are you?"

"Engine room. No sign of Pilon or Jadak."

"Keep looking. We're about ready to go."

"Major," Carter whispered into his walkie-talkie, "what's our status?"

"We might have it. We've got it down to two wires . . . one blue, one white. We're testing."

"How long, man?"

"Sir, it's impossible to tell."

Carter thought. They didn't have time. El Adwan was getting nervous.

"Major, if the tanks blow, how long do we have before the ship goes down?"

"Probably a good twenty minutes, sir."

Time enough to get the crew out, Carter thought.

"Major, run a bypass and pick a wire. Is everyone else on?" There was a series of affirmative answers. "All right, everyone with your night glasses on. Chief Harris?"

"Here, sir."

"Get ready to cut the generators."

"Ready, sir."

The wait went on for minutes. Carter could see that El Adwan was beginning to sniff the wind.

Then the word came.

"Culham here, sir. We've run a bypass. I'm guessing blue. When we cut, it's twenty seconds."

"Go, Major," Carter growled, in his mind seeing everyone ready to take out their targets.

"It's a cut," Culham hissed.

Carter—and, he was sure, all the SAS men—were

sweating out a pound a second. He forced himself not to blink as he watched the sweep-second hand of his watch.

". . . nineteen . . . twenty . . . twenty-one. . . . Good guess, Major. Chief Harris?"

"Yes, sir?"

"Kill the lights. Everybody . . . *go!*"

The instant the lights went dead, Carter opened up with the Sten on full automatic. Carefully, he kept his fire away from the captain.

It had the desired result.

El Adwan fired a burst in reply, and reached for the pulser. When nothing happened, and Carter's slug from a new magazine started finding his range, he leaped from the hatch.

The Killmaster dropped to the next deck and gave chase.

El Adwan fired until his magazine was empty, then he discarded the AK-47. Now he was on the main deck and running aft, with Carter still firing.

MacCreedy appeared before him and El Adwan veered left into the officers' quarters. Just as he did, one of Carter's slugs caught him in the thigh.

Carter dived through the hatch into the officers' mess. El Adwan was against the far bulkhead, a pistol held in both hands.

"Give it up, Adwan," the Killmaster hissed. "By now all your people are dead or captured." Carter could see El Adwan's face in the moonlight through the big portholes.

"I know that voice . . . you're Carter."

"That's right."

The man laughed. "God, you don't give up, do you!"

"Never. Hang it up."

The face changed. The gun lowered and hit the deck.

"Sure, why not?"

Carter wasn't surprised. He had almost expected it.
Calmly, the man pulled out a cigarette case. He lit a long
brown cigarette and smiled.

"They'll try me and probably get a conviction. But do
you know what, Carter? They'll give me five years . . .
at the most. Any more than that and you'll have hijackings
all over the world to get me out. And I won't even do
the five years. Some government will want to make a
deal with another government, and part of it will be my
release . . ."

Carter watched the smirking face and listened to the
glib talk. And as he listened, he knew the man was right.
The trial would take two years, a couple of million dollars,
and he would be convicted.

And two years later, Abu El Adwan would be out.

Carter pressed the trigger on the Sten and kept pressing
until the magazine was empty.

Then he walked back out on deck. Colonel MacCreedy
was waiting.

"No casualties on our side, sir. And the officers and
crew are safe."

"And theirs?" Carter asked.

"Thirteen accounted for—eleven men, two women—
all dead."

"No," the Killmaster said. "Fourteen . . . all dead."

DON'T MISS THE NEXT NEW
NICK CARTER SPY THRILLER

LETHAL PREY

Carter moved like a snake, coming up from the floor to strike. He lunged at the guard in the corridor, pushing him against the other cell, depending on Al Jabbar to take care of him. He turned in one fluid movement, lunged through the celldoor as the other guard was bringing his rifle to bear, and caught him under the chin with the heel of one shoe.

The guard went down, but he was a bull of a man and was only stunned. He shook his head, picked up his rifle by the barrel, and swung it at Carter.

As Carter prepared to take him on, he was distracted by the scuffle in the corridor. Al Jabbar was having a difficult time holding the first guard, and the other prisoners were not helping him. While the Killmaster glanced over his shoulder, the second guard swung his rifle, catching Carter a glancing blow in the head, taking him down.

The guard advanced, reversing his rifle. Before he shot, he aimed a kick at the supine American, catching him in the ribs and raising him a foot off the floor. Carter fell back, almost unconscious.

But then two of the hillmen Carter had fought lent a hand and grappled with the guard while Carter tried to regain his wits. Even in his dazed state, Carter knew that if he and Al Jabbar were caught at this, it would be the end of freedom for sure.

The first guard had broken free and in a blind fury turned to fire at Al Jabbar. The hillmen were all over the second guard. Another prisoner in Carter's cell lunged at the door to take on the first guard.

The guard in the corridor swung his gun and fired. The slugs lifted his attacker off his feet and flung him backward into the cell. He crashed into the guard and the other hillman, who were still struggling over the rifle. Just as his blood-soaked body slammed into them, they were caught up in the gunfire. The first guard's finger was frozen on his trigger in a frenzy of fear.

Carter was off to one side and below the line of fire. His head cleared fast as he saw the carnage. The second guard, the hillman, and a half-dozen prisoners had gone down under the wicked hail of fire. The Killmaster lunged up and to one side, taking the first guard in the gut with an iron fist just as the hammer of his rifle clicked on empty.

That had done it. Carter could hear the booted feet and shouts of other guards in a far corridor. He grabbed the keys from the fallen guard and opened Al Jabbar's cell.

"Don't follow us for five minutes," he shouted to the other prisoners. "If you do, you're dead."

He ran into the cell for the dead guard's gun just as two other guards rounded the corner. He loosed a short burst, catching one of them in the gut while the other sought shelter around a corner.

"Come on!" he growled to Al Jabbar. "We can't let them get organized!"

He kept the submachine gun pointed at the corner of the corridor where he'd last seen the guard. As they came up to it, they saw him disappear around another corner.

"Our only chance is to keep after him and surprise any other guards on duty," Carter rasped to Al Jabbar as he stuck his head around another corner.

The fleeing guard was fumbling with keys in a locked passage door. Carter let him get the door open, then fired low, sweeping the guard's legs from under him.

They rushed to the open gate. Carter threw the wounded guard's weapon at Al Jabbar and continued down the maze of corridors to the open air and freedom. He had memorized the route on the way in. He knew of only one more corridor, one locked door, one stairway, and an upper hallway between them and the outside.

A guard stood at the last locked door, an old M-15 clutched in his hand. A fat man, his belly protruding over his tightly cinched belt, he shook from head to foot as he stood, paralyzed.

They advanced cautiously. The man was frozen on the spot, his rifle in hands rigid with fear. Carter butt-ended him on the chin with his rifle. He went down like a beached whale, his head striking the concrete, the sound echoing hollowly in the deserted corridor.

Al Jabbar was getting into the spirit of the fight. Almost before the man had struck the floor, the Tunisian was on him, had the ring of keys from his belt, and attacked the door furiously.

They were through. Only the stairs and the upper hall remained before the outer door was available to them.

The stairs were long and dark. Carter peeked around the corner and saw no one. He started up the stairs. He could hear muffled shouts above. Halfway up, with Al Jabbar against the right wall, emulating him, two men appeared at the top with handguns blazing.

The escaping men had no choice. They both opened fire on full automatic and blasted the two men back.

They raced for the top of the stairs. No one was around. The wooden hall was slick with blood and the walls were like a surrealistic painting, the thick red liquid still dripping downward.

They could smell the fresh night air drifting in from an open door. Carter turned to the source of the draft and led his friend to a glass-enclosed front entrance.

One man sat in a chair behind a desk, isolated from the noise below. His head was nodding, his chin almost on his chest. Al Jabbar dealt a hard blow to the back of the man's head with his rifle as Carter grabbed a handful of keys from a rack behind the desk.

"You'll be faster at this than I will," Carter yelled at his friend as they headed for the parking lot. "Pick out a couple of cars, drive one to the center of town, and take a taxi to the villa. Be damned sure it's secure before you alert your guard."

He waited for what seemed like hours as Al Jabbar matched up the keys with two unmarked police cars. He threw a set of keys at Carter and pointed to a car.

"I'll take my time," Carter yelled into the night wind. "If the villa is not secure, hang back in the shadows and look for my taxi."

As he swung the car around, another car entered the lot, a submachine gun sticking from one window. One of the guards must have telephoned for help before Carter reached him.

Carter turned his car in a tight circle, then braked behind the intruder, well out of range of the machine gun. He snatched up the gun on the seat beside him as Al Jabbar's car sped past, then emptied his clip into the other car's gas tank.

An orange and red mushroom of flame erupted, enveloping the police car and the men in it. Carter tossed the rifle out the window and floored the accelerator as his car tore out into the night.

—From LETHAL PREY
A New Nick Carter Spy Thriller
From Jove in May 1988

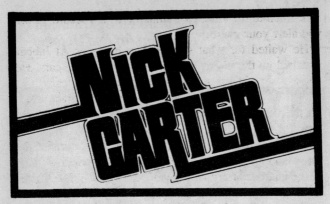

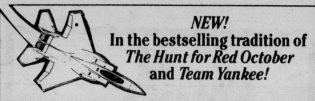